S0-BCT-816

"Did you want to kiss me, up there in your bedroom?" he asked her.

"I think I did, actually," she admitted. "But I know that was stupid."

"I don't know what this is, but we can't keep dancing around it, can we?" he said.

Sadie swallowed. "We should do exactly that—just keep dancing." She forced herself to say the words. Talking about it would only lead to her admitting that she had a huge and ever-growing crush on her best friend.

"We *have* to talk about it, Sadie, because we both know something's going on here. I can't even think straight around you anymore. Something happened when I got back from Boston…"

"Nothing happened, Owen, and nothing *will* ever happen," she snapped, begging her eyes not to give away her raging desire. No one had ever looked at her like he was looking at her now. He never wanted to talk about anything serious, and the fact that he did now, about *them*, fired her up and sent the fear of God rushing through her all at once.

Dear Reader,

I love a good best-friends-to-lovers romance. Maybe that's because I had a good guy friend once who I thought might one day become something more. It was scary and exciting, feeling those feelings bubbling up.

Sadly time and geography came between us, but I often wonder what might have happened if I had pursued it.

I may have snuck some old personal fears and feelings into this one, which makes Sadie and Owen's story one of my favorites yet. I hope you enjoy it. And if you have a friend you haven't declared your true feelings for, I hope you someday summon the courage to tell them! What do you have to lose?

Love,

Becky

HIGHLAND FLING
WITH HER BEST FRIEND

———

BECKY WICKS

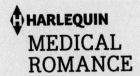

HARLEQUIN

MEDICAL
ROMANCE

If you purchased this book without a cover you should be aware that this book is stolen property. It was reported as "unsold and destroyed" to the publisher, and neither the author nor the publisher has received any payment for this "stripped book."

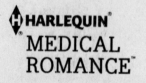

HARLEQUIN®

MEDICAL ROMANCE™

Recycling programs for this product may not exist in your area.

ISBN-13: 978-1-335-73772-4

Highland Fling with Her Best Friend

Copyright © 2023 by Becky Wicks

All rights reserved. No part of this book may be used or reproduced in any manner whatsoever without written permission except in the case of brief quotations embodied in critical articles and reviews.

This is a work of fiction. Names, characters, places and incidents are either the product of the author's imagination or are used fictitiously. Any resemblance to actual persons, living or dead, businesses, companies, events or locales is entirely coincidental.

For questions and comments about the quality of this book, please contact us at CustomerService@Harlequin.com.

Harlequin Enterprises ULC
22 Adelaide St. West, 41st Floor
Toronto, Ontario M5H 4E3, Canada
www.Harlequin.com

Printed in U.S.A.

Born in the UK, **Becky Wicks** has suffered interminable wanderlust from an early age. She's lived and worked all over the world, from London to Dubai, Sydney, Bali, New York City and Amsterdam. She's written for the likes of *GQ*, *Hello!*, *Fabulous* and *Time Out*, a host of YA romance, plus three travel memoirs—*Burqalicious*, *Balilicious* and *Latinalicious* (HarperCollins Australia). Now she blends travel with romance for Harlequin and loves every minute! Tweet her @bex_wicks and subscribe at beckywicks.com.

Books by Becky Wicks

Harlequin Medical Romance

Tempted by Her Hot-Shot Doc
From Doctor to Daddy
Enticed by Her Island Billionaire
Falling Again for the Animal Whisperer
Fling with the Children's Heart Doctor
White Christmas with Her Millionaire Doc
A Princess in Naples
The Vet's Escape to Paradise

Visit the Author Profile page at Harlequin.com.

For the one who got away.
You know who you are.

**Praise for
Becky Wicks**

"Absolutely entertaining, fast-paced and a story
I couldn't put down…. Overall, Ms. Wicks has
delivered a wonderful read in this book where the
chemistry between this couple was strong; the
romance was delightful and special."
—*Harlequin Junkie* on *From Doctor to Daddy*

CHAPTER ONE

Just an hour and a half from Glasgow, the Isle of Bute is a gorgeous island in the Firth of Clyde, where the hips and haws and the hum of the bees are all that interrupts the stillness...'

A CLATTER FROM the kitchen made Sadie look up from her laptop. Her good friend of a decade, Owen Penner, was bent over with his nose in her fridge, looking for something she'd probably forgotten to buy at the supermarket.

She carried on reading the guidebook, grateful it was a Saturday morning and they had nowhere else to be.

'It says here it's largely ignored by travellers to Scotland, who arguably miss its abundance of Scottish Isle beauty. Do you know how quiet it's going to be there, Owen, compared to Chapel Hill...or Boston? Are you sure you're ready for it?'

'Where's the orange juice?' He was distracted.

'There isn't any.'

'There's always orange juice at your place.'

Sadie tutted. 'Callum bought that, remember? Not me. Owen, it doesn't sound like you're very excited to be taking this position in literally two weeks' time...'

'Of course I'm serious.' Owen's tone changed abruptly as he closed the fridge and marched to her dramatically like a military soldier. 'Checking in with full attention, Commander Mills.' He saluted, sliding his six-foot frame back into the dining chair beside her.

Sadie pulled her newly styled honey-toned waves tighter into their ponytail, biting back a smile as his cologne hit her nostrils, plus that unmistakeable Owen smell—the personalised scent she'd missed the whole time he'd been gone in America, studying the intricacies of functional neurology and adding it to his repertoire. He might be one of London's top neurologists, and undoubtedly had one of the biggest brains she'd ever known, but Owen was still a man. Therefore he sometimes found it tough to multitask.

She'd never admit it, least of all to him, but if you looked beyond the chiselled cheekbones and sculpted nose, and the wicked gleaming brown eyes that drove his female conquests crazy, he was still kind of an adorable kid in a buff adult's body.

His biceps told her he'd spent a lot of his time

in Boston working out at an expensive gym with the rest of the fit American colleagues she'd seen on his social media, and now that it was coming on for spring, he probably knew how good he looked in a new green shirt that she'd never seen before.

She'd complimented him on it. Men these days didn't get enough compliments, which she'd read wasn't good for their mental health—an area of huge importance and interest to her since...well, since her brother's death. So she'd been making an effort to change that lately.

Not that it had changed anything with Callum.

It hit her with a jolt of pride that the sound of her ex's name on her lips just now, and the thought of him leaving the flat with her beloved Larry the cactus, wasn't still causing rafts of anger and humiliation and fear to bowl her over—not like it had done before. Thankfully Owen had returned home after his year away just days after the break-up, which had helped things immensely. But...*ugh*. Four years wasted.

Four years of planning a life with Callum Mc-Farley, all for him to tell her, *'It's just not working out. I don't feel a connection any more,'* right before she was due to leave for her coveted placement at Rothesay Recovery.

The high-end facility developed treatment plans to directly address each emotional, physical and psychological issue of its patients. She'd been all set to take a six-month placement in the role of occupational health consultant there, amongst the world's most exclusive clientele, all of whom were paying an absolute fortune to stay at Rothesay. After the break-up, though, she'd almost backed out.

The facility was so remote. She'd had a feeling all that silence would wreck her head, and she wanted to be her very best self for her patients. If it hadn't been for Owen suddenly announcing he wanted to go too, she would have cancelled.

'So, show me more testimonials,' Owen said now, his coffee steaming up his glasses.

She slid the laptop over to him and watched as he used his T-shirt to wipe the lenses before he leaned closer to read the testimonials from satisfied patients against a backdrop of the towering, castle-like mansion that housed the exclusive Rothesay Recovery.

She still couldn't quite believe they were *both* going to be working there. Together. Before he'd left to boost his career in the US, he'd worked at St Thomas's Hospital, while she'd been consulting at various places around London as usual. They'd actually never worked in the same facility before. And heading to this craggy, windswept part of Scotland's west coast would be a world away from his former plan to take a well-earned break from work altogether in Thailand.

'Southeast Asia will still be there later,' he'd told her, when she'd asked him why he'd give that up to go to Scotland with her.

But hadn't he said that nothing had ever worked him harder than the American health system?

'It's not the kind of island you had in mind when you showed me that resort on Kho Samui,' she said, testing him further now, studying the hilly background to the text alongside him. This page detailed the comprehensive treatments offered in this safe haven for high-profile, high-net-worth individuals who were struggling with various physical and mental health issues.

'It sounds like you don't actually want me to go,' he said, feigning a sorrowful look. 'You don't have to worry, Sadie, I'm committed.'

'That'll be a first.' She couldn't help a sly eye-roll—her way of teasing him, of course, no malicious harm meant.

Owen perched his glasses back onto his nose slowly and played with his phone for a second. For some reason the look that crossed his face at her words sent a spiky shard of ice through her heart.

'I'm teasing you,' she reassured him quickly.

He merely shrugged, and she felt worse.

Now that she thought about it, this notorious playboy who was her best friend in this entire city—OK, maybe in the entire world—hadn't mentioned being with anyone in a while. If he'd met anyone in America, he hadn't said so.

But seriously… Did she need to bring up the stream of women he usually enjoyed hovering around him like dogs in heat? She'd given up trying to meet his girlfriends over the years because they never lasted more than five minutes. He didn't do relationships—which was his prerogative, she reminded herself. Not everyone was like her. Serial monogamy was *her* trademark.

Sadie watched his handsome profile as he clicked through the website. Then he asked her what she was smiling at.

'You're so paranoid,' she said, nudging him, flushing.

She'd been thinking about how he had arms like a superhero now and wondering—with the strangest twinge of jealousy—how many women must have swooned over his British accent in America.

But she had also been thinking how proud she was to call one of London's most highly rated neurologists her friend. Owen might be a player in his personal life, but he was a hero in his profession. He'd saved more lives than he'd admit—humble as he was, at least when it came to his career.

While conventional neurology was designed

to spot diseases and pathology, often it couldn't properly diagnose a problem unless it was already advanced. Owen had come back from Boston one of the most qualified doctors in his profession. He was now equipped to advise and treat people searching for treatments alternative to what traditional neurology might offer them. He could identify which areas of the brain were compromised and figure out how to fix them, and do it all with the same effervescent charm that had always made countless people fall in love with him.

She was probably the only woman in their circle of friends he'd never hit on.

Gosh, it was ten whole years ago now since they'd met at Imperial College, she thought, accepting his offer of a cup of coffee and watching his tall frame as he slunk across the kitchen in his socks to get it for her. He'd accidentally flicked a pen in her direction back then, and had got blue ink all over her white jeans. She'd yelled at him. He'd apologised, bought her lunch, talked her ear off, and made her laugh—and also wonder how it was they'd never spoken to each other before that. They'd been four years into their seven-year course, after all. But then, she'd been a bit of a loner for a long time, grieving for Chris, her brother.

She straightened her back, seeing Owen glancing at her sideways, probably trying to read her mind. He often looked at her the way he was doing now, when she was quiet.

Owen had been instrumental in urging her out of her shell again after they'd become friends aged twenty-two, but even now, ten years later, she still felt like a shadow of the person she'd been before Chris had died.

'Like I said, it's going to be very quiet there,' she reminded him now, pushing thoughts of the past away with a mental broomstick and motioning to the screen before he could ask what was on her mind.

Scotland was exactly what she needed, for many reasons.

'Maybe some quiet will be good for me,' Owen replied with a shrug, but he was still looking at her with interest.

Owen didn't know much about Chris—not all the details anyway. Certainly not the fact that her brother had taken his own life. When the topic of his recent death had come up not long after they'd met she'd let him think it was an accident. Her grief had been all-consuming then, even four years after the event, and talking about it with Owen had been the last thing she'd wanted.

But he'd swept into her life and eased the suffering almost instantly. In fact, Owen Penner was still the friend she called when jokes and light-heartedness were required.

So her brother had loaded up on booze and steered his motorbike into a quarry right before she was due to start her course at Imperial College… So her parents had got a sad, quiet divorce while she was burying herself in her studies… It didn't mean she had to burden other people with her past, or have her issues picked apart and analysed.

She should've been a better sister—yes. She should've noticed sooner that her fun-loving, free-spirited brother had started showing signs of depleting mental health. She should have noticed her own parents slipping further and further apart after his death. But she hadn't seen any of it.

Sometimes she thought that maybe her career choice was an inevitable product of her trying to assuage the guilt she felt over Chris's death. Psychiatry hadn't felt like a great fit—she'd wanted to study something more diverse—but assessing patients' mental health was vital in her consultancy practice now, and she saw a part of herself—and Chris—in every patient.

'Will I need a kilt?' Owen asked now, breaking into her thoughts.

She snorted, imagining it suddenly. He'd look hot in a kilt. Really hot.

Why was she suddenly thinking things like this about Owen?

Because you missed him, she reminded herself, *and you appreciate him, that's all.*

She'd been three seconds away from withdrawing her application for the occupational health consultant placement at Rothesay Recovery the night Owen had offered to apply there too—they'd still had a placement of the same length for a neurologist open at the time.

'Why don't I go with you?'

He'd said it so matter-of-factly, right there and then over the takeaway he'd bought her, as if he didn't even have to think about it.

'Unless you really don't want me jumping in on your dream role?'

'Why would I mind?' she'd replied, quickly. It hadn't even crossed her mind to mind—only that he might not actually mean it.

God, she'd missed him when he'd left for America. Things hadn't been quite the same without him around.

'We've never been anywhere together outside of London, really, have we?' she said now, sipping her coffee, studying the three-day growth darkening his jawline.

He looked good with a bit of a beard, and a hint of his thirty-two years in the one or two flecks of grey she knew he hated. Owen was, without a doubt, the most physically attractive man she'd ever met. Callum—slimmer, shorter, never quite as successful, though not through lack of trying—had been intimidated by their friendship sometimes.

Make that the whole time, she thought now, remembering one afternoon out on the river in Richmond, when Callum had accused Owen of being in love with her. She and Owen had been having another one of their 'accent competitions', in which they competed to see who could do the best accents from around the world. Callum had called it stupid. Owen had rolled his eyes in her direction and whispered something in a very bad Mancunian accent and Callum had just exploded at both of them. Totally ruined the mood.

Owen had hooked up with some girl from Malaysia that very night in a pub. While she'd been in another corner, saying whatever she could to placate Callum on the subject of what he called her 'blatant flirting' with Owen.

That particular hook-up had been Owen's way of proving to Callum he in no way wanted *her* as another notch on his bedpost. She knew that much. But when he'd ended things, less than a week later, Owen had also been showing everyone—yet again—that he definitely wasn't the relationship type. He was there for all the fun, but Owen Penner just didn't fall in love. He didn't commit to anyone. It wasn't *him*. And that was fine by her. She knew where she stood with Owen and that was all that mattered.

Owen's eyes were still narrowed, as if he was

trying to remember somewhere they'd been together that wasn't London. Of course *she* remembered everywhere they'd ever been together. Just
as their relationship had never gone beyond the
friend zone, their friendship had never gone beyond Zone Five.

They talked on about the clients they might
meet, and the fishing they might do in the lake
on the Rothesay estate, and as the hours passed,
as they always did so easily in his company, she
allowed a little bubble of excitement to ripple
through her nerves.

'You've never been fishing in your life, Owen!'

'Well, *you've* never hiked up anything higher
than Primrose Hill, Sadie.'

He pulled his *Shrek* face at her then, which
made his chin curl up into his neck while he bit
on his lip, and she sniggered into her cup, thinking, as she always did, that even when he tried
to look ugly he couldn't.

She and Owen had fun wherever they went.
Why should Scotland be any different? Mind
you...they might have more alone time together
there, she and Owen. Would their friendship be
tested? she wondered suddenly, studying his
slender fingers on the laptop keys. Didn't remote living test people?

What about all those wilderness programmes
on the telly, about people forced apart by difficult circumstances. She would never do anything

to put her friendship with Owen at risk—*ever*.
God knew she'd already lost enough important
people in her life. To lose him too would be un-
acceptable.

CHAPTER TWO

OWEN SHRUGGED FURTHER into his jacket and scarf as the seagulls dived and darted at the front of the ferry from Wemyss Bay to Rothesay, the main town on the Isle of Bute. For a moment he imagined himself on a sunny beach in Thailand, cocktail in hand, the shadows of swaying palms playing across his shirtless chest, and wondered if he'd made a huge mistake.

But one look at Sadie huddled into her own scarf reminded him that he'd rather be in cold and rainy Scotland with her than lounging in Thai sunbeams with anyone else. They always had fun.

Besides, it wasn't *actually* raining...yet. It probably would soon enough, despite the current spring vibes. Scotland wasn't exactly renowned for its excellent climate and it was cold even now, in late March. But it was beautiful, and Sadie was beautiful, and everything was working out just fine.

He caught himself. What was he doing, thinking things like *Sadie is beautiful*?

Of course she was beautiful—that was an undisputed, undeniable fact, as pointless to observe as *Scotland is Scottish*.

'Look how gorgeous it is,' Sadie enthused with a slight squeal, looking around from behind her oversized sunglasses.

The smart Victorian buildings lining the seafront in Rothesay were bursting into view now, pretty as the postcard his mother had used to keep on the fridge. The water was as blue as it was in Thailand. He could even see trees that looked suspiciously like palms.

'It's exactly how I imagined,' she said. 'I can't believe we're actually here, Owen. I thought you might at least be *thinking* about changing your mind.'

Owen chewed on his cheek and stared at a strand of honey-brown hair blowing free from her ponytail around her face. He'd thought about it, yes, but his heart would never have let him. The thought of his hard-working, loyal and recently heartbroken friend of ten years missing out on an opportunity like this because of an idiot like Callum made his blood boil. The only choice had been to come with her.

'I had to see the home of whisky and haggis for myself,' he said. 'Otherwise you'd just try to show me on your phone, and we both know you take terrible photos.'

Sadie smiled and told him she was serious, and grateful. Then she looked at her feet, and sniffed self-consciously, as if she didn't know how to handle a man who actually stuck to his word.

So Callum was finally out of the picture. Good riddance. Of course it was only a matter of time before she gave that giant heart of hers away to someone else. She always seemed to be in a long-term thing with someone…almost as if she was afraid to be alone. The opposite of himself, he thought. She didn't exactly *need* a man, either, as far as he was concerned.

Sadie was one of the highest-rated UK-based consultants in occupational medicine. A client had sent 'thank-you' flowers to her door just this morning, right before she'd handed her keys over to the new renter and they caught the train to Glasgow. Proud wasn't the word for what he felt about her. She was winning at life on her own.

Sadie Mills knew how to reach people and make a legitimate, positive difference to their lives, just like he did. He wasn't going to blow his own trumpet, but he knew, professionally, that they were going to do good things where they were going.

They met their driver at the ferry port. A man called Caleb, who helped with their bags. Sadie had somehow packed the world into a sky-blue suitcase almost twice the size of his.

It suddenly occurred to him how remote they were actually going to be, living in a part of the nineteenth-century mansion that housed Rothesay Recovery, treating up to twelve live-in patients. They'd be joining fifteen other specialists who would cater to their wealthy clients' unique needs. The other specialists and staff would be on site, living and working alongside them, but on his days off he planned to explore the forests, take naked dips in idyllic lakes and embark on scenic walks through the Lowlands and Highlands by way of a few whisky distilleries. Alone.

It wasn't as if there would be any options in the hook-up department all the way out here. And Sadie was more fun than any of them had ever turned out to be, anyway.

He'd kind of missed her in America. He'd gone to her place the second after he'd ditched his bags at home, and she'd looked at him through her hair all night, eyeing up his new muscles even when she was sniffling over Callum dumping her.

His colleagues in Boston had liked the gym and he'd grown to like it too. Going there had turned out to be a better use of his time than chatting up women—none of them had been Sadie. He'd started to anticipate their weekly Sunday video calls. He'd even turned down a few dates to stay at home and talk to Sadie—

especially after she'd hinted that she might be leaving for Rothesay right after he returned. That hadn't sat well with him. He'd been looking forward to spending time with his best friend after being away for so long.

And now here he was. Along for the ride.

A shiver of anticipation tickled his spine as they slid into the back seat of the taxi. This was it. No backing out now. The six-month stint wasn't going to be the holiday he'd planned, for sure. He knew enough about private live-in residencies to know they involved some of the toughest work out there, but he was ready for the challenge…and so was Sadie.

It was a short three-mile drive to Rothesay Recovery.

'Working at Rothesay Recovery, huh?' the driver said. 'I heard a rumour that that actor's in there now. You know the one whose son died in that movie stunt?'

'Conall McCaskill?'

Sadie threw Owen a look that made him direct his smirk out of the window—she was clearly starstruck.

'That's the one.'

She pushed her sunglasses up onto her head and squeezed his knee. Owen cleared his throat, noting her hand on his jeans, her newly trimmed, polish-free manicure. They hadn't been told who the residents were yet. He'd assumed they'd have to sign NDAs when they arrived.

'So sad…what happened,' Caleb muttered, shaking his head. 'I heard he turned to the bottle pretty bad. You pair might have your work cut out with that one.'

Owen listened as Caleb made grand assumptions about the A-list Scottish actor, noting the sunlight in Sadie's hair. *You pair.* Did this guy Caleb think they were a couple? Lots of people did, but it had never happened. Not in this life anyway.

It *could* have happened. At least, he had tried once. He could be back on that dance floor in his mind in seconds if he wanted, but he tried not to think about it too much because… Well, what was the point?

He'd been young and drunk when she'd put him in his place, not long after they'd met. They'd been dancing in that cheesy club, Sylvester's, and she'd kept looking at him strangely, as if she was thinking something wicked. But the second he'd leaned in to act on it she'd sped from the dance floor like a meteor. Neither of them had ever mentioned it again.

It would have ruined their friendship, so it was probably better that nothing had happened. He would have messed it up anyway, if they'd got together. Much as he would now, probably. Getting into something serious was not on his radar—not with anyone, and especially not with a friend like her.

He found his jaw was clicking now, as he pictured that day on the boat in Richmond when Callum had outright accused him of being in love with Sadie. They'd only been having a laugh, like they always did, doing some silly accents or something. He'd laughed off the accusation, just as Sadie had. But that night in the pub he'd overheard them arguing. Sadie had said it over and over again.

'Owen is just a friend! That's all he will ever be, trust me.'

At the time he'd wondered why it had stung so much. It was the truth, after all. But it sounded like something his mother might have encouraged people to think—the woman who'd birthed him and then regretted it. In Josephine Penner's eyes the Penner men were useless, and her rage over his dad's incessant philandering had sealed his own fate, he supposed. He was never going to get himself into anything he couldn't get out of... There would be no wedding bells, no babies, no mortgages and trips to IKEA. No, thanks—not for him. All that couples' stuff only wound up in misery for everyone involved.

Maybe it was best he'd been shut down long ago by Sadie. Now they were purely friends—simple, no complications. Just the way he liked it.

'I've read about that hotel.'

Sadie cut into his thoughts. He realised he'd been staring at her face again, while she'd been looking at a spooky hotel outside. The Scottish sunlight made the blush on her cheekbones even pinker. She rolled down the window. The air smelled sweet and fresh, rolling in over her familiar perfume.

The Glenburn Hotel looked eerily empty.

'Looks like the perfect setting for a ghost story,' he said aloud.

Caleb bobbed his ginger head from behind the wheel. 'Aye, you're not wrong, lad. Plenty of ghosts around here—especially where you're going.'

'Stop it!' Sadie gasped. 'There are no ghosts where we're going... Are there?'

'There's talk of a Lady in White,' the driver replied.

Owen nudged her gently, grinning at the look on her pretty face. 'You don't believe in ghosts, do you?'

'Stop it,' she said again, and nudged him back harder, which prompted an attack of poking fingers on each other and laughter between them.

Sadie cleared her throat as Owen pushed her hand away from his ribcage one last time, registering as he did so just how hard his heart was bucking in his chest. Caleb was rolling his eyes, mouthing the word 'flirts'. But it certainly wasn't flirting. He and Sadie didn't *do* flirting. At least he would never do it. He knew how she viewed him. How could he forget?

He took in the trees and the wildflowers through the car windows as they drove, and found himself thinking, as he often did when it was quiet, about all the things he'd never told Sadie. Or anyone.

Like how, as a kid, he'd got to know the wobble of his mum's chin and what it meant—usually that she was about to spend some time sobbing behind the bolted bathroom door. The meltdowns often came right after his dad had left for some sudden meeting or appointment that they all knew had nothing to do with the business his parents had built together from the ground up.

If it hadn't for him coming along, maybe his mum never would have married his dad and ruined her life. If she hadn't tied herself to the man so irrevocably, in so many ways, maybe she wouldn't have felt obliged to stick around and endure all the lies and belittling put-downs and bitterness. Either way, he'd learned over the years exactly when to leave someone—*before* things had even the remotest chance of becoming serious.

Sometimes he got confused about Sadie—because he was a guy, he supposed, and because she was a beautiful, smart, thoughtful and successful woman, who had to all intents and purposes come to trust him. They'd come to rely on each other through the years. Neither of them was particularly family-orientated—at least she barely ever mentioned her divorced parents, and her brother had died in a motorbike accident the summer before she'd started university. She didn't ever talk about it. He didn't ask.

Sadie was independent, like him. Ambitious, like him. He respected her. Needed her, actually. Her kindness, her insights, her ability to cheer him up without ever being mean. Every other woman came and went. He would never risk losing Sadie's friendship—not for anything. She was irrefutably the best thing in his life.

'Here we are!'

Caleb was steering the taxi up to some giant arched iron gates. He jumped out of the car to press a button and within seconds they were rolling up the long, sweeping driveway. Sadie made that excited squealing noise again and gripped Owen's arm, and he tried to ignore a sudden lightning bolt that seemed to strike him at her touch. The same one he'd started to feel back in Boston, seeing his screen light up with her face...

'Look at that water feature! Ooh, check out that glasshouse—that must be the Victorian fernery... I can't believe these turrets... It looks just like a castle...'

Her being so excited was infectious. Owen smiled to himself. Thailand felt further away than ever, but this was definitely going to be interesting. The house was huge. All fishtail slated turrets and leaded crests, and bay windows with balustraded parapets.

A black-haired lad with a side parting met them in the grand entrance hall. He wore a smart white uniform and his badge read *Fergal: Welcome Host*. Owen watched the way Sadie looked the man up and down, then found himself catching her arm as another guy in the same white uniform wheeled their cases away across the chequered black and white floor. She shot him a look of surprise when he put his hand on her elbow, and he swiftly removed it, wondering why he'd felt the sudden need to have every ounce of her attention.

Stepping into professional mode, Owen made sure he looked suitably impressed as they were given a tour. It wasn't difficult to be impressed.

'The house dates back to about 1844, and the grounds extend to roughly three acres, including our therapeutic Victorian glass-covered fernery,' Fergal said, proudly. 'Our residents like that. In fact, they're all in there now, because it's potting hour. You can see the bay from your suites, I believe, and the golf course. But the best rooms are kept for our paying guests, of course.'

'Of course,' Owen echoed. He cocked an eyebrow at Sadie behind Fergal's back and mouthed

Potting hour? incredulously. She frowned at him, as if to say, *'Behave!'* But her lips twitched.

'Your rooms are on the second floor in the right-hand wing,' Fergal explained in his thick Glasgow accent as he led them up a grandiose staircase.

This time it was Sadie's turn to arch an eyebrow. She mouthed the word *Wing?* at him, while pulling a face, and he laughed, then turned it into a cough. Luckily their 'welcome host' was too wrapped up in impressing them to notice.

'I'll show you your rooms later, but first Dr Calhoun would like to meet with you.'

On the landing, Fergal swung open a huge wooden door and ushered them both inside the room onto thick olive-green carpet. Owen felt the tingling heat from Sadie's shoulder creep along his arm and excite his senses as they found themselves standing side by side before Senior Clinical Co-ordinator and CEO, Dr Christine Calhoun. In a setting like this, it felt like coming face to face with the Lady of the Manor.

'Welcome, Dr Penner, Dr Mills.' Dr Calhoun stood and smiled from behind a huge oakwood desk.

Her white teeth gleamed between thin lips as Owen shook the fifty-something doctor's hand.

'We feel lucky to have you both here,' she said in a distinctive Glaswegian accent, glancing between him and Sadie with interest, as if sizing them up in person.

Was she wondering if they were a couple too?

'Let's get to business, shall we? There are a few things you should know now you're here, that we couldn't discuss on the phone.'

'Is this about Conall McCaskill?' Sadie asked, folding her arms in her smart suit jacket. She was almost as tall as Calhoun in her heels.

Dr Calhoun shot her a slightly guarded look as she motioned them to sit. Quickly she produced the expected non-disclosure agreement forms from a creaking drawer, and placed them down in front of them.

'We can't keep a whole lot secret around here—not even with the blacked-out windows on our transport,' she informed them wearily. 'Mr McCaskill is on the premises, yes, you have heard correctly—along with quite an interesting intake. In fact, we're relying on you to help us make the breakthrough Maeve… Mrs McCaskill…is hoping for from him. So far he's refused to speak with anyone, or even acknowledge his own PTSD. The team is excited about your credentials—both of you.'

Sadie turned to Owen, a look of steely determination flashing in her eyes. It fired him up on the spot, as if she'd shot liquid adrenaline into his veins. Then she crossed her legs and turned back to Calhoun, all business.

'You'd better fill us in, Doctor,' she said.

CHAPTER THREE

'MR MCCASKILL?' SADIE tapped her nails on the open door, two steps ahead of Owen.

Conall McCaskill was sitting in silence in a leather armchair by the floor-to-ceiling windows of his immaculate modern suite. Maybe it was his grief, or the leaf-brown V-neck sweater and dark army style trousers he wore, but he looked older in person than she'd imagined somehow.

Behind him the bathroom door was ajar, revealing a giant Bird of Paradise plant in a terracotta pot and a French rolltop bath with claw feet. It was luxury compared to their own rooms. Not that hers was bad. She just hadn't slept well, thanks to an old pipe, somewhere she hadn't been able to locate, that just wouldn't stop banging.

Owen pulled two chairs up, one either side of Conall McCaskill's and fixed a smile to his freshly shaven face. 'How are you today, sir?'

Charm personified.

Sadie took the other seat and smirked, remembering catching him taking a selfie earlier, on the staircase. She'd done the same just moments earlier. Their uniforms were vastly different from what they were used to. Nothing like their regular white coats. In her case it was a fitted cream skirt and a sleek white shirt emblazoned with the gold-embroidered *RR* logo. Owen wore a smart white dress shirt and cream dress trousers that hugged his bum just right...

What? She caught herself. Why was she thinking about Owen's bum right now?

There was something about him, she realised suddenly. Something she'd missed while he'd been in America. She couldn't put her finger on it... *And neither should you want to*, she reminded herself. She was simply glad to have him back, and for the chance for them to work together for the first time. Their friendship was going to make them a great team.

Still, he did have an incredibly cute backside...

'We're doing the rounds...introducing ourselves. We're the new recruits. I'm Owen Penner, and this is Sadie Mills.'

Silence. Conall McCaskill still had his gaze fixed on the statue of the mermaid guarding the fountain outside the window. Sadie crossed her legs and adjusted her watch, reining in her thoughts of Owen's...physical attributes.

She'd dealt with this kind of thing before. PTSD developed differently in everyone. But never in her dreams had she imagined she'd see it in the hero of her favourite childhood action movie *Surrender*.

If she'd known Conall McCaskill was on the residents' list before this she would have re-watched that movie. Or maybe that would have made this situation more difficult, she thought, studying his famous sloping nose and square jaw.

She and Owen could have watched it together, she supposed, her with her feet up on his lap, the comfy way they'd watched movies together since their Imperial College days. Well, apart from that time when Callum had caught them and instructed Owen crossly to keep to his own side of the sofa.

Owen started explaining what their roles would be. He was to discover what might be ex-acerbating Conall McCaskill's problems and help develop a strategy for calming any overactive areas of the brain. She was to help him regain his purpose in life, so to speak, by helping him with daily life skills and hopefully getting him back to peak performance in society—maybe even in another movie.

It was going to be a challenge. But then, it sounded as if the first psychologist he'd been to hadn't known what to make of his situation at all. Dr Calhoun told them he'd been sent there by someone from the film company's insurance provider. The notes stated that Mr McCaskill was dressed nicely and was well-groomed for his appointments, when in fact, according to Maeve, his wife, he hadn't showered in days and had gone in wearing the same jeans and stained sweater he'd been wearing for a week.

It was Maeve—famous in her own right—who'd insisted he see someone 'professional'. Hence Rothesay Recovery, and them.

The sullen-looking A-list film star looked like a completely different man from the accredited actor she'd grown up watching on screen. And, just as they'd been warned, he didn't seem too warm about the idea of them being there.

'I don't want any help.'

Conall McCaskill's gruff Scottish bark shocked her. This was not the confident, kick-ass, muscled gym addict she'd seen on her TV. He was only in his mid-sixties, but his son's tragic death had clearly aged him in many ways.

'We know you've been through a terrible tragedy—' she started.

'Well, you should—it was all over the Internet. Didn't even take them an hour to get the photos out there after they took Scott's body away.'

Sadie drew a breath. A breeze from the open window ruffled the actor's grey-streaked hair.

'It was a stunt that went wrong,' Owen stated next.

He was looking at the notes, which wasn't entirely necessary—they'd both read all about it when it had happened. Six months later it was still cropping up from time to time on the news—the stunt co-ordinator's legal trial was ongoing.

Scott McCaskill, Conall's thirty-two-year-old son, a movie stuntman, had been filling in for his father in a chase scene when the brakes had failed on the car he was driving. The poor guy had collided with a tree and the tree had won. A fake explosion had turned into a real one, which had probably finished him off, although no one really knew. Conall had seen it happen.

'We understand you haven't really had a chance to deal with it all,' Sadie said now, crossing her legs in his direction and noting, just for a millisecond, the actor's liquid blue eyes flash over her knees in the sheer pink tights. 'It must have been difficult to escape and get some privacy...'

'Why do you think they put me in here?' he snapped.

More silence.

Owen stood up and crossed to the window.

Sadie found she was holding her breath again.

Another long pause.

'I remember when I first watched you in *Surrender*,' Owen said.

He crossed his arms in his crisp white shirt, studying the mermaid statue, while Sadie wondered exactly how many hours he'd put into the gym to get biceps like that. How had he even found time for the numerous dates he must have been on while he was in Boston? He still hadn't talked to her about them.

'I knew you were a real hero, even back then.'

'DC Shawn was my *character*—i.e. not me,' snapped Conall.

'Yes. But around the same time you did that commercial to save the dogs in Vietnam. Right after that my friend's mother had to drive her to the cinema to put a bid on a cardboard cut-out of your character. There was a queue there already. Everybody wanted you—the *real* you, the Puppy Ambassador—in their living room.'

'Not any more.'

'Nothing's changed out there,' Owen assured him, and Sadie blinked.

That had been her mum who'd done that for her. She must have told Owen and forgotten. She barely spoke about her family to anyone. It hurt too much to think about how good things had been before Chris died. But the Puppy Ambassador—how could she have forgotten that?

She shuffled closer to Conall McCaskill on her seat, shooting Owen a look. 'I remember donating my pocket money to the cause,' she said. 'If my dad could see me now, he'd tell me to remind you how you made me want to get a dog. Of course we weren't allowed one—not even after my brother begged for one...'

She trailed off, straightening up on the seat. Conall McCaskill was frowning, as if waiting for her to finish. Even worse, Owen was looking at her sympathetically, which rattled her defences instantly. This was not the time or place. Why had she brought up her brother? Conall McCaskill was making her nervous.

'I wasn't allowed to watch *Surrender* unless I'd tidied my room first,' she said quickly, raking a hand through her loose hair. 'That's power, sir. No one else could get me to do that—'

'She's right about that,' Owen interrupted. 'She's the messiest person I've ever met.'

Sadie's mouth fell open. If they'd been anywhere else she would have play-punched him. But to her surprise Conall McCaskill's face softened. Only slightly, but there was an undeniable shift in his mood.

Damn, Owen was good. Buttering up a celeb's ego was probably the only place to start with any kind of treatment, and Owen had realised that immediately. Just the tiniest crack would do to loosen him up—then they could slip into his psyche and start with the real work. And trust Owen to lighten the mood, like he always did.

She'd address his comment about her messiness later, she decided, as Owen continued talking about his friend transporting the DC Shawn cut-out home in her mum's car, how his cardboard head had stuck out through the back window for the whole ride.

Maybe she'd let her standards slip a little since

the break-up with Callum. Owen had certainly done her washing up a few times, while she'd been sniffling into a pot of ice-cream on the sofa, feeling sorry for herself. Once, he'd even made her bed for her. She'd stood there, bleary-eyed, watching him from the doorway, while he'd propped up her childhood teddy bear and talked about making her comfy, thinking how even Callum had never made the bed. He'd always waited for her to do it.

'What's the deal with you two anyway?' Conall McCaskill asked now, turning his head back to her.

She realised she'd been looking at Owen in the sunlight, noticing again how good he looked in his uniform. It would have been so different here if he hadn't come too.

'What do you mean?' Owen asked evasively.

'You know what I mean. Are they sending couples here now? I know they've had a few singles who thought it was too remote. They wound up leaving the island.'

'We're not a couple,' she said quickly, as her heart lurched in her chest. 'We're simply colleagues and friends who've known each other a long time.'

Conall McCaskill scanned her from her chin up to her hair, his familiar close-set blue eyes roving her face as if he was looking for a reason to mistrust her. Owen was frowning, seemingly memorising the mermaid's scales in the garden.

She quickly changed the subject to the actor's treatment plan, explaining her planned series of daily hand-eye co-ordination exercises in addition to a strict dietary regime, which often helped PTSD patients more than it had been previously thought, according to some new research Owen had studied and implemented in the States.

'Colleagues and friends, huh?' mumbled Conall McCaskill, halfway through retying his shoelaces, as if that was better than addressing the difficulties she was observing in his ability to do so without cursing.

'That's correct.' Sadie stood up, allowing him the dignity of continuing without them looking, wondering why his scrutiny had unnerved her. Maybe she was just starstruck. This man was a Hollywood icon. She could think of several people who'd lose their minds if she told them she was caring for this megastar on his road to recovery.

Owen turned. 'We're here for *you*, sir,' he added, although it was Sadie he was looking at now.

In a flash she remembered the look in his eyes that had set her defences on fire before, the sympathy in his gaze after she'd mentioned her brother. If he was here because he felt sorry for her in any way…because of her brother, or Callum, or anything…

No. Surely not. Not Owen. Owen did things for Owen. Always.

Except when he's taking care of me… Then he's the least selfish person I know. Women have come and gone in his life, but he's always been there for me.

Sadie pushed the strange new revelation from her head before it could develop into questions pertaining to their strictly platonic relationship status. Meeting Conall McCaskill was getting to her, that was all.

Next on their rounds was Mr Vivek Kumar, a wealthy businessman who sat wringing his hands, his eyes all over the place.

'I can still hear the sound of the ice cracking under my head,' Mr Kumar explained, making Sadie's heart hurt for the man.

He'd slipped on some icy steps on a business trip to Colorado last winter and hurt his head. He had experienced difficulties in speaking and co-ordination ever since.

Sadie felt Owen's eyes on her the whole time she was assessing his ability to follow instructions, walking in various directions around the room. Every time he turned left instead of right her heart sank further, but Owen was making furious notes, and she knew he was devising a plan of his own that they'd incorporate into a healing schedule.

Again, the thrill of working with him to help a patient through a traumatic brain injury gave her a boost—although unfortunately so did remembering the way he'd put his arm around her shoulders this morning. Just for a second, by way of saying hello on the landing. It had sent a bolt of electric heat through her loins that had taken her quite by surprise. He'd ruffled her hair awkwardly afterwards, as if to turn his affection into something he might also show a puppy dog, and she'd blushed all the way to breakfast.

'How did you sleep last night?'

Owen had caught her up on their way into the fernery for potting hour.

'Why?' she asked him, noting that the patient they'd just assessed, forty-eight-year-old Portia DeMagio, was pressing a hand to her forehead ahead of them in the humid domed glasshouse.

Sadie frowned. She'd suggested Portia stay inside, as she'd mentioned feeling a little unwell, but Portia had insisted on getting some air.

The slight, smartly dressed sexologist, who lived in Edinburgh with her film director husband, was here to get to the bottom of her cluster headaches, which had been diagnosed as 'episodic'. Her illness was characterised by periods of weeks or months of attacks, alternated with pain-free periods. With surgical intervention ruled out already, Sadie was adjusting Portia's existing programme for coping with and hopefully reducing the ferocity of her debilitating headaches.

It really was a diverse list of live-in residents, but only two were here for potting hour. The others were attending a yoga class—with the exception of Conall McCaskill, who'd refused to join in with anything today.

'I just wondered if you'd heard anything in the night,' Owen said now, keeping his eyes on Vivek Kumar, who was settling his large, round, portly self into a seat at the glass table set amongst the ferns and flowers.

'Now that you mention it, there was something banging all night. A door or a pipe or something,' she said.

She noted how Mr Kumar was struggling with sitting too far away from the table, and then too close to Portia for his comfort. They'd concluded by now that his spatial awareness was very much impaired. Sadie helped him with his chair, and luckily Portia just smiled.

'I couldn't find where the noise was coming from.'

'I heard that too.'

Owen scratched his chin thoughtfully. His room was right next to hers, so she wasn't surprised.

'I thought maybe there was a window open in your room.'

'*My* room? Why would I leave a window open?'

'That's what I thought.' He leaned into her and lowered his voice, grinning. His mouth tickled her ear. 'Maybe it was the ghost.'

'Stop it,' she hissed.

Parminder, a trainee care assistant, looked up from her distribution of shovels and tiny plastic pots of shrubs, which were to be re-planted in peace and quiet.

'Stop what?' she asked, raising her perfect neat brows as they approached.

And Sadie had already caught her looking a little too long and hard at Owen—which annoyed her more than she wanted it to. It was up to Owen what he did and with whom—why should she care? Just because he had possibly come here for her, and not just for 'the challenge', like he'd said, it didn't mean he owed her his full attention all the time. It was probably only a matter of time before he noticed Parminder's crush, if he hadn't already.

Why am I so annoyed by something that hasn't even happened?

'I was saying we think there's a ghost in our wing,' Owen told Parminder.

Vivek rolled his sleepy hooded eyes. 'There's no such thing as ghosts.'

'Exactly,' Sadie replied, taking the heavy iron

seat next to Owen's and picking up a small shovel. 'Owen was just messing around.'

She waggled the shovel in his direction, laughing despite her strange mood when he pretended to swipe it from her hand.

Parminder cleared her throat…flicked her gaze between them nervously. 'I saw something in the garden my first night here,' she said, sounding a little embarrassed.

Owen put the shovel down and shot Sadie a sideways glance.

'At first I thought it was one of the residents, but it was after-hours, and they always lock the doors at night.'

'It was probably the caretaker,' Sadie said, nudging Owen's foot under the table.

'In a long white dress?'

Sadie swallowed—just as a bird landed on the glass dome above her and made her jump. Ghosts weren't real, but still… The thought of encountering anything paranormal here turned her stomach inside out.

'Lots of people wear long white dresses,' she said casually, digging her shovel into a mini plant pot in an attempt to calm her pulse. 'Even Owen here wore one once. Remember that Halloween party at Imperial? When you went as a corpse bride?'

Owen sniggered. Vivek and Parminder looked at them with interest, giving them the same kind of look that Conall McCaskill had given them earlier.

'You guys went to college together?' Parminder asked curiously.

Sadie nodded, chin raised, wondering why she suddenly felt more territorial over Owen than a guard dog on duty.

She was just about to regale them with another funny story about Owen when Portia DeMagio clutched her head again, dropped her shovel to the floor, and promptly fell face-forward into her plant pot.

'Oh, my God! What…? What…?'

Vivek was on his feet before anyone could move, but Owen urged him back into his seat while Sadie and Parminder gently lifted Portia from the soil and readjusted her in the chair. Her mouth was wide open.

'She's out cold.' Owen frowned, coming forward and checking her eyes while Sadie wiped the mud from her cheeks.

If only Portia had listened to her earlier and stayed in the main house when her symptoms had started.

'She told me she can usually tell when an attack this bad is about to happen,' she whispered at Owen.

'She shouldn't be blacking out on the meds she's taking,' he replied.

Parminder was on her radio. In less than a

minute someone was rushing down the path towards them with oxygen. Portia was already blinking, coming to on her own, even as they slipped the oxygen mask over her face. She was most apologetic for fainting, but Owen wasn't having any of it.

'We're rescheduling our next one-to-one, Portia,' he told her sternly as Sadie noted a fresh and telling sheen of perspiration on the woman's forehead. 'We need to get you off those meds. They're clearly not working.'

'Nothing's worked so far. That's why my husband sent me here,' she managed through her mask.

Sadie watched the woman grasp Owen's hand and squeeze it with a strength that defied her size and current situation. She'd mentioned her husband 'sending' her here to her too, in an earlier session.

ª"We both will,' Owen replied. 'That's why we're here.'

Sadie stood back with Vivek and Parminder as Owen helped Portia all the way up the gravel path, past the mermaid, till they were out of sight. The poor woman spouted far too many apologies the whole way, and Sadie wondered how she'd been coping with events like this so far. Embarrassing, humiliating, debilitating...

Did her husband think this was his last resort? Sending her to this place? How many times had he scraped Portia off floors and carpets while fearing for his beautiful wife's life?

Cluster headaches weren't life-threatening, but another sufferer had once described them to her as *'Like your brain is being attacked by an angry elf with a machete'*. She wanted to help Portia. She *would* help. She and Owen would work together to make sure of it.

She would also have to work on not noticing Owen's impressive physique as much, she decided. How dare he come back from Boston looking hotter than ever…distracting her like this? Thoughts like that needed to be nipped in the bud pronto, before he caught her and started thinking she *liked* him, or something!

As if.

CHAPTER FOUR

BY THE END of the second week Owen had got pretty comfortable with a fishing line in his spare time, but he still felt as if Conall McCaskill was the one who was getting away. No matter how hard he tried to get him to talk in their sessions, the depressed actor used only grunts by way of conversation, and insisted on staring right past him for the most part, officiously offering to tell him the time, as if they needed confirmation that he didn't want to give them any more of his.

It was almost as infuriating as his new attraction to Sadie.

Maybe it was working with her…watching her in action around the patients. The way she'd been with Portia since the incident in the fernery was nothing short of dedicated. She'd sat with her every evening since, when she was reading and journaling in her room, making sure she wasn't alone long enough for another headache to creep up unannounced—which it hadn't, thankfully.

Maybe it was having her close again after so

long away from her…or the fact he hadn't had sex in a while…but he'd had a dream about her last night. The kind of dream that would not stop playing on his mind.

Owen cast his line over the side of the little boat while Rothesay Recovery loomed large in the sweeping estate beyond. Only his, Sadie's and Conall's fishing lines were disturbing the ripples of the blue lake. Of course Sadie had to be looking cute as hell in her uniform of a white shirt with a cream jacket and matching fitted skirt—her body was as fine as her brain.

Yes, focus on her brain, he reminded himself in annoyance, frowning into the lake. Her body was off-limits. Unlike the way it had been in that dream. Even thinking about it was torture.

But then, he'd rather think about *anything* other than his father right now. And the way he had casually announced his new engagement at the end of their recent phone call—as if it was more of an afterthought than a big deal.

Owen felt his jaw lock again. It *was* a big deal. *Jay Penner strikes again.* The ink was barely dry on his latest divorce papers. What would this Michaela woman be? His fourth wife? Fifth? He was losing track.

'So, have you done much fishing before?'

Sadie's voice broke into his thoughts. She was trying to make small talk with Conall from the other side of the boat they'd managed to coerce him onto.

'A few times with my co-star on *Ascension 2*,' was McCaskill's simple, bored response.

Owen fought not to intervene. His role this morning was to observe the actor's mood and motor skills in activities like this, now he'd put him on a new anti-inflammatory diet. Conall hadn't had an alcoholic drink in over a month, but Owen suspected his previous diet hadn't helped his PTSD.

Post-traumatic stress was a wicked beast. Sometimes he saw hints of it in his mother—caused by none other than his father, of course. Although she hadn't exactly distanced herself from him, or done anything to try and help her situation. The woman was the very definition of a martyr.

Jay Penner had walked out on the two of them when Owen was eleven, in favour of some woman he'd met on a first-class flight back from Hong Kong—Edwina. Every new relationship and marriage since then had merely put another knife through her wounds.

It didn't help that neither would step down from the business they'd built together. On the surface, everything was about Leap—the ground-breaking web design platform for which they were co-founder and CEO jointly. Underneath… Who knew? His mother seemed to prefer being tortured rather than admit her own stubbornness and pride, and her unadulterated loathing of his father was a mask for a damaging kind of undying love for the man…bordering on the masochistic, in fact.

'Catching any sea monsters over there, Owen?' Sadie called, eliciting another grunt from Conall as she tossed her own line over the side with a yell a lot like a noisy tennis player might emit.

'Not so many,' he replied, momentarily forgetting his annoyance as he noticed her new sunglasses. They suited her. Then again, Sadie looked good in everything.

When he'd mentioned to his dad that he was here in Scotland on a placement with her, he'd heard a low murmur of approval in the back of his throat—Jay Penner's way of ranking a woman highly in the looks department. Dad must have seen photos of them together on his social media over the years, although Owen had managed to keep him away from her in person— more out of embarrassment than anything else.

Owen listened to Sadie and Conall making awkward, stunted small talk while his father crept in and out of his thoughts. The guy could push his buttons, for sure—it was a lost battle for him not to get wound up over the way he treated marriages like throwaway takeout containers.

His mum would probably call any time now, he thought, checking his phone. She'd tell him the same thing she always did: *'Don't you dare do anything to ruin anyone like your father ruined me!'*

She loved to impose her self-righteous opinions on him. The things he'd heard from her over the years still made him cringe. How the Penners—his grandfather and great-grandfather included—were notorious for having too much money and not enough morals…how she'd thought she'd be the one to make his dad into a one-woman guy…how stupid that had been because no one ever would.

His mother was *still* paying for her mistakes… still regretting getting in too deep. Regretting getting serious with his father, walking down the aisle and making babies with him.

Sadie's squeal drew his attention back to her. Her line had bounced back and hooked into her hair. Biting back a smile, he put his line down and crossed the boat to help. He wasn't great at fishing, but she was worse.

'What are you like?' he whispered as his fingers found the hook amongst her thick honey hair and untangled it gently.

'Thank you. I can do it,' she muttered suddenly, catching his fingers just as they went back in to smooth her hair down.

He tried to discern what the new scent was lingering in his nostrils. He sniffed again—lavender. The oil was in every female's room at

Rothesay. He'd seen the diffusers in a session with Portia.

Embarrassment flashed in Sadie's eyes as she glanced from him to a smirking Conall and he retracted his hand—*why had he done that?*

'I don't think the fish need to worry with you around,' Owen said, clearing his throat.

'Very funny,' she replied, trying and failing to hide her face behind her hair. Her cheeks were flaming ruby-red in the sunlight.

What the hell was that?

Conall was grinning at them. 'Did I ever tell you how I met my wife?' he asked suddenly.

'No, you didn't,' Sadie replied, flustered, before Owen could say a word. She shuffled back to the side of the boat and resumed her hopeless fishing.

'She was a production assistant on one of my movies. Cutest girl around for miles…wicked sense of humour.'

Conall's eyes found Owen's as he said it, as if they were sharing some kind of moment.

'Maeve was the only one on set who treated me like a human being and not some star who needed special attention. I appreciated that.'

Owen wound out his line. He didn't need to ask why Conall was mentioning his wife here and now. Clearly he was insinuating he and Sadie had some kind of husband-and-wife-type interaction going on—which wasn't entirely untrue, he supposed. They weren't having sex, for a start. Didn't marriage kill that kind of thing?

Wild passion withered. Attraction always faded.

He frowned at the water, remembering how his mother had verbally bashed his 'useless' father even while they were still together…even at the cost of making things deeply uncomfortable for him and any unsuspecting school friend he'd happened to invite to the dinner table.

'I can't believe Maeve sent me here,' Conall said gruffly. 'Of all people…'

'She wants you to get better,' Sadie told him gently.

'She's grieving herself. I told her she should come here too.'

She wasn't drinking herself into a heap every night, Owen wanted to say.

But instead he chose to listen while Sadie asked him more about his early encounters with Maeve. He knew she was dying to know. And they both knew Conall McCaskill's anhedonia—an inability to express any kind of pleasure—must have been making his wife's life a misery.

Maeve McCaskill had given up 'the biz' years ago, to launch a successful line of luxury cooking items and cook-books, promoted largely on her YouTube channel. She was a big hit on all social media, apparently, always cooking, and talking about how to use this particular air fryer or that tin for a batch of muffins—not that he paid much attention to things like that.

Unlike Sadie.

Sadie even had one of her aprons.

She'd always looked ridiculously cute in the pink frilly fifties-style thing—like a sexy housewife or something. One time, when they'd both had too much of her girly gin and elderberry mix, she'd danced around her kitchen while she was wearing it, and he'd had to stop himself taking the husband-and-wife game too far by hoisting her up onto the counter.

Owen cursed himself. Now he was imagining what sex with Sadie would be like up against the kitchen counter. It wasn't as if he'd *never* imagined it—even before the dream. He was a guy, after all. She'd just never go there with him— obviously. And he wouldn't initiate it. She'd accuse him of wanting to make her another notch on his bedpost, which he'd never do with someone like her.

If his mother ever met Sadie—which he'd been trying to avoid—she'd only take him aside and remind him of all the things he shouldn't do. Tell him not to ruin her. She might even tell Sadie what she loved to tell anyone else who'd listen— how his father and pretty much all the Penner men were useless. The shame and embarrassment he felt just thinking of her hearing all that caused a fire in his blood. He knew Sadie's approval of him was imperative.

She was professionally perfect to all who encountered her, but behind the scenes she was special—to him, at least—because she made no pretence about who she really was. Not like some of those girls who'd approached him in Boston…the ones he'd wound up going to the gym to avoid…

'Isn't that right, Owen?'

'Huh?' Owen turned. Sadie was scanning his face quizzically.

'I was saying to Mr McCaskill that he should invite his wife here for the annual gala that was coming up. You know…the event they've put up all the posters for?'

Owen vaguely recalled seeing some posters about the place.

'He doesn't think she'd want to come,' she continued.

'Why wouldn't she want to come?' Owen asked, catching Sadie's look. She was letting him know she was fishing for information as much as for the perch that were hiding somewhere in the water below them all.

It was interesting, seeing her studying this troubled man. Every half-smile, every grunt and sigh, was a piece of the actor's story, unscripted. He was telling her how she could help him without even realising it himself.

'Is it that you think she wouldn't want to come? Or do you just not want her to see you in this place?' Sadie asked him carefully. 'There's nothing to be ashamed of, you know. Everyone needs help sometimes.'

Silence.

Tension filled the cool morning air as Conall's face grew tight and sullen. His eyes darkened as he clenched a fist at his side. 'You know nothing about what we've been through,' he growled at them. 'Get me off this boat.'

'Mr Mc—'

Without a beat Owen stepped between Conall and Sadie. The look in the guy's eyes was not unlike the look on his character DC Shawn's face, right before he launched a hand grenade at an approaching battleship.

'Sir, if you'd just—'

'I said, *get me off this boat!*'

McCaskill's lips grew pursed and small, and his eyes went black as a thunderstorm. One look at his dilated pupils told Owen it was obvious their fishing trip was over. They'd pushed him too far.

Owen could almost feel Sadie's disappointment through the light squeeze of her fingers around his wrist.

'OK, we're going back,' he said quickly, reading her signal. 'Sadie, do you want to steer or shall I?'

* * *

Half an hour later they'd deposited Conall on the small wooden jetty with Parminder and were back on the boat on the lake—just the two of them. With two hours before their next appointments, Owen had offered to show Sadie a few fishing skills, despite her insisting he had none himself.

She was very quiet, though. Obviously she was still thinking about Conall...or maybe even that weird moment between them earlier...

No, surely not. Sadie had probably forgotten that already.

'He's been off the booze for a while, but the anhedonia is still going strong,' she was saying, with her rod dangled over the side, the sunlight still playing in her hair.

'I know that,' he said, rolling his eyes.

'It's not something *you've* ever had a problem with,' she responded.

Her eyes were twinkling now, but Owen bristled. 'Depends what kind of expression of pleasure we're talking about,' he replied, tossing his own line over the boat a little harder than he'd intended.

Sadie studied his face, eyes narrowed. 'What did I say?'

'You assume too much about me, Sadie Mills,' he answered.

She scoffed. 'I don't assume anything. You're a pleasure-seeker.'

'And what's so wrong with that?'

Sadie opened her mouth to reply, but closed it again, as if she regretted it already, and he bit back the words he was about to say as well. It wasn't worth it.

Or maybe it was. Too many people already assumed he was just like his father, and maybe they were right. At least, they *used* to be right, he corrected himself. When was the last time he'd been with a woman? He couldn't even remember now. His heart hadn't been in it for ages. He'd been too busy missing Sadie from afar.

'If you mean I seek out the good things in life—like spending time with *you*, like being here, trying to make a difference to these people's lives—then, yeah, I'm a pleasure-seeker. But if you mean I just sleep around...'

'But...you do. Don't you?'

'Not any more, if you must know.'

'I'm sorry.' Sadie flung her line out and frowned defensively at the water.

Great. Now he felt like an idiot for making a big deal out of her teasing him—but she might as well have lashed his nerve-endings with a million little whips. Maybe she still saw him the same way she had when they were in their twenties, but he *had* changed. It wasn't that he wanted to settle down, specifically, but he was definitely a lot more discerning about who he gave his time and attention to.

She didn't know that, though, looking at him here, where she'd stuck him years ago, in the friend zone. She didn't know how much he'd missed her. Maybe he hadn't realised the extent of it himself till he'd come home, he realised suddenly.

The silky strands of Sadie's hair blew out on the breeze and tickled his cheek, and he felt the oddest sense of being out of his depth, even with the shoreline right ahead of him.

'I'm sorry,' she said again, softer now. 'Owen, what's really bothering you? You've been weird all morning.'

'My dad's just winding me up,' he said quickly.

No point dissecting these feelings right now... or ever.

'Why?'

'He's getting married. Again.'

Owen was about to elaborate when his phone rang again. His mother.

Sadie's eyes burned into his back the whole time he was talking. As predicted, his mother was furious, but he knew the wobble of her voice by now, and all the things she wasn't saying underneath her irritation. She was heartbroken all over again.

'He'll chew this woman up and spit her out like he did to me—like he did to Edwina, and

Abigail. He's like a kid with a shiny new toy. I hope you never treat anyone like that, Owen…'

'Mum, you know what he's like. What do you want me to say?'

Sadie steered the boat back to the jetty after he'd ended the call. They both knew their fishing trip was over for a second time.

'Do you want to talk about it?' she asked, as he tied the boat's ropes to a post on the jetty.

The morning sun showed no sign of disappearing behind the famous Scottish rain clouds, but that conversation had sapped every inch of his own sparkle.

'I don't think there's much to talk about,' he told her tightly. 'He's always been this way. Done with one woman—on to the next. Maybe it runs in the family, huh?'

He said the last part rhetorically, under his breath, but she heard and caught at his arm.

'Owen, I really didn't mean what I said before. I don't know why I even said it. I haven't heard you talk about anyone in a while now. Was there no one in America…?'

Her voice faltered slightly as she asked the question. It caught him off-guard. Was that a twinge of discomfort at having to ask him such a thing?

'No,' he replied, searching her face.

Something strangely alien hovered between them as she held his gaze, then looked away.

'I know I've never met him, but I'm sure you're nothing like your dad,' she said quickly. 'Is your mum OK?'

'She'll be fine…she's used to it,' he replied, pulling his arm back.

His heart drummed incessantly as he headed up the gravel path.

Sadie followed him. 'How many wives has your dad had, exactly, Owen? You've never actually said.'

'Too many,' he replied, realising that till now he'd been too embarrassed even to talk about it with her.

He exhaled deeply, curling his fists into his pockets for a moment. He shouldn't be venting to Sadie like this…but she'd been unnerving him lately, and the boat had been small, and she'd heard his mother's words just now, even though she hadn't been on speakerphone. Humiliation was encroaching upon his cool, and it was not a nice feeling.

'I don't know why, but it's like Mum's still in love with him. Can you believe that?'

He expected her to laugh—the thought was insane, after all—but Sadie's eyes narrowed as she studied him. Then she shrugged. 'I don't know… I guess being in love is powerful, right?'

'Being in love is a waste of time,' he shot back.

He expected her to roll her eyes, the way she

usually did when it came to his opinions on anything regarding romance, but this time she didn't.

'You just don't want anyone to know how wonderful you really are,' she said on a sigh, sending his heart crashing into his ribs. 'I see that, Owen. And love is not a waste of time. Maybe you've just never let yourself feel it.'

'Oh? And you have?' Her nonchalance was infuriating. 'What about Callum? You guys never had anything in common—nothing at all, Sadie. Did you ever even love him for real, or were you just looking for a comfort blanket?'

The hurtful words were out before he'd had time to think. He stepped towards her, cursing himself. 'Sadie, damn it. I'm sorry...'

'Whatever. I haven't got time for this.' Sadie slipped from his reach, put her hands in the air and marched on past him, up towards the house.

Owen let her go, oscillating between annoyance, helplessness and confusion. She'd launched a truth bomb at him out of nowhere and he'd reacted by pushing her away—which was the last thing he really wanted.

What was going on between them lately? Maybe he should give her space, he decided. His father's news was getting to him more than he knew.

CHAPTER FIVE

'So, spill it. What's the deal with you and Owen?
You're practically giving off sparks.'

Portia DeMagio was looking down her nose at
Sadie over her glasses, and she hoped she'd man-
age to convey non-comprehension, even as her
pulse spiked at the sexologist's keen observation.

'Just now…before he left the room—you
should have seen the way he looked at you. But
you're ignoring him. Outside of these sessions,
I mean. What did he do?'

'This session is about you, not me,' Sadie reminded her, with a smile she was sure hadn't
made it to her eyes.

What look had he given her?

'Now, walk me through this week's journal
entries,' she told Portia. 'I see you've been noting what you've been eating and drinking before
the headaches start?'

'Yes. Owen's plan is already making a notice-
able difference. His lovely face always helps, too.
Am I right?' Portia shot her a sideways smile

and kept her hands on top of the journal, tapping her fingers on the closed book. 'Come on! I see something's going on between you two.'

'We're not going there,' Sadie replied quickly, trying and failing to take the journal from the stubborn woman.

'Don't be offended. Reading people is my job.' Portia informed her, who was looking radiant in a red shirt and black trousers.

'It's *my* job to focus on you,' Sadie told her patient gently, and finally managed to extract the journal from her hands.

Together they went over her entries for the week, and discussed how Owen's cold laser therapy and new electrical muscle stimulation programme, combined with a plant-based diet, was already helping to reduce the severity of her headaches. Sadie was showing her how to stretch out any tight muscles that might be contributing to her headaches, and advising hot yoga, which Portia was insisting Sadie join in with.

There were regular yoga sessions here at Rothesay Recovery. Maybe they *all* needed some time out in a Zen space, Sadie thought. Her mind would not stop slipping back to that stupid heated encounter by the lake a week ago.

She was still fuming at the way Owen had spoken to her about Callum, saying what he'd obviously been dying to say since the break-up. The person she'd considered her closest ally had accused her of keeping a comfort blanket as a boyfriend!

You're only annoyed because he's right, the voice in her head kept telling her.

'Are you sure you're not going to give me at least a snippet?' Portia wheedled, looking up from her journal. 'If you won't tell me what he's done, start at the start. How did you meet?'

'At college.'

'Have you ever kissed?'

Sadie snorted, feeling her cheeks flame at the question. 'Absolutely not.'

'But you've thought about it. I can tell.'

Sadie sat back in her swivel chair and sighed. Thoughts of kissing Owen raced like poisoned arrows through her brain, faster than she could stop them. But it was no good thinking stuff like this…she'd stopped doing that years ago, after that ill-fated night at Sylvester's.

'You *have*—there's no point denying it!' Portia looked delighted. 'Heck, honey, even *I* have. He's a catch.'

Realising she wasn't going to let it go, and also maybe feeling a little comforted by Portia's profession, Sadie found herself wanting to tell her. What was the harm?

'Actually…there was one time we might have come close…'

They'd not long met. Her group of friends had made plans to hit a cheesy dance club called

Sylvester's, and she'd invited Owen along, too. She could still remember the adrenaline, walking into the club with its throbbing music and flickering neon lights, and seeing his handsome face light up, as if he'd been waiting just for her. She'd contemplated that maybe, just maybe, they might take their burgeoning friendship to the next level that night. They'd been dancing around some kind of strange attraction for a couple of months by then, at least.

But, being her, she'd been so nervous about the prospect, and the huge potential for rejection and/or heartbreak, that she'd lost count of exactly how many cocktails she'd poured down her neck. After getting hideously hammered she'd run off to be sick—and woken up the next morning with a severe hangover and even more severe memory loss.

She was glad that she hadn't done anything stupid. It wasn't as if she'd ever had a one-night stand, and she certainly shouldn't have started that night—with Owen, of all people! She'd simply had a momentary lapse of judgement and forgotten he was entirely unsuitable boyfriend material.

Also, she must have been a total idiot when she was drunk, because he'd done a disappearing act for several weeks after that.

A vague recollection of running from the dance floor had sneaked up on her from time to time, and another one of crawling into a taxi alone. She'd been so utterly embarrassed about the whole night that she'd never mentioned it again. Neither had Owen. In fact, the next time she'd seen him after that, she'd simply said sorry. And he'd said the same back. And, while she had never been entirely sure what *he* was sorry for, she'd decided it was far less humiliating to forget about it and stay friends.

'So, you admit you were attracted to him once upon a time?' Portia was twirling one of her artfully designed earrings around her finger, fascinated.

Sadie snapped back to the present. This wasn't very professional, she realised, but then, nobody here much cared for the regular way of doing things, and opening up to her patients often paid dividends when they did the same to her. If only Conall McCaskill would crack just a little more...

'At one time, yes, I suppose I felt some attraction,' she admitted. 'But we were young. It's different now.'

'You're good friends, aren't you?' Portia mused.

'Yes. Exactly. *Friends.*'

'We should always be friends with our lovers.'

'Maybe if we're living in a romcom...sure. Now, can we talk about *you*, please? How did you meet your husband?'

Portia's expression darkened. *Uh-oh.* Sadie

had a feeling the husband was still in this woman's bad books, for sending her here.

'We were indeed friends before we were lovers,' she said wistfully, after a moment. 'We had sex as an experiment—can you believe that? To see if we had chemistry. I dared him, thinking he'd turn me down. Don't ever assume a man will turn down sex, even if he *is* just your friend.'

She huffed a laugh as Sadie opened the journal and swivelled her chair closer, trying not to think about having sex with Owen. Although now she was, and her throat had turned into the Sahara Desert. Having his big new-muscled arms locked around her would feel like the ultimate definition of protection, and there was nothing that turned her on more than a guy who could make her feel safe.

'And now you're married,' she said, fanning out her hair and pressing a hand briefly to her hot neck.

'And now he's sent me here,' Portia replied acidly.

'Because he loves you.'

'He does love me...' She sighed, softening slightly, as if she was finally coming to terms with the fact that it might have pained her husband to send her here as much as it had hurt her. 'You know, it's funny. When I'm angry with him I want to have sex with him even more. This is the longest we've ever been apart...and celibate.'

Sadie bit back a laugh. She couldn't imagine experiencing that amount of passion. She'd certainly never had angry sex with anyone, and probably never would. Sex for her was always nice...kind of standard, she supposed. Never particularly passionate or exciting, just something you did in a relationship once or twice a month.

How embarrassing it was that she'd dared to accuse Owen of never letting himself feel real love.

She was used to blocking out the fact that she'd always chosen safety and security over real, burning passion, thanks to losing both after losing Chris. But wouldn't it be nice...wouldn't it be everything...to feel safe as well as sexy, and wanted, and in love. *Really* in love.

Portia was watching her closely. 'When Stan and I fight, we can go at it four, five, even six times a night,' she said. 'Get yourself a man who you can fight with, Dr Mills. Do you and Owen ever fight?'

Sadie cleared her throat. 'Um...not really,' she said, turning back to the journal, her mind spinning.

She and Owen had never had a disagreement at all before coming here. But she did feel that spark between them, if she was totally honest.

She'd felt it when she opened the door to him after he'd come back from America. He'd pulled her in tight and breathed in her hair on the doorstep, as if the smell of her shampoo was giving him life, and she'd cried in his arms, half over Callum, half in relief at having Owen home and all to herself.

She'd felt it on the lake, when he'd pulled that fish hook out of her hair tenderly, almost lovingly, just like a boyfriend would.

Things had been changing between them ever since he'd come back from America—it was pointless to deny it. But knowing what she knew about him now—how affected he'd been by his parents his whole life—his resistance to relationships made a lot more sense.

He would never give her what she needed.

All the more reason not to let these new feelings marinate, she decided resolutely.

Hours later, alone in her room, Sadie turned another page of her novel and failed, yet again, to take in what was happening in the story.

Owen hadn't come back yet. She'd been listening out for the familiar creak of his door, the sound of the key turning that always told her when he was back in his room. But it was already ten-thirty p.m., and still no sign of him.

Ugh. Maybe he was avoiding her after their altercation by the lake.

Putting her book down, she stared out of the window. Was he really still angry with her for the pleasure-seeker comment? It was clearly her fault they'd argued, but he'd pushed her buttons too.

'Sadie?'

A quiet knock on her door made her leap from the bed so fast she almost tripped over her shoes. Owen's mouth was right up against the door outside—she could see his shadow underneath.

'Are you awake?' he whispered.

Opening the door, she forced herself to look sleepier than she was, having been lying awake, wondering where he was. Seeing him in jeans and his familiar burgundy hoodie sent a warm wave rippling through her, but she crossed her arms over her dress and cardigan to refrain from hugging him.

'Awake,' she confirmed. 'What's up?'

'Are we still in a fight?' he asked, cocking an eyebrow.

She bit back a smile. 'No.'

'Good, because that was boring. I have something to show you.'

Owen took her hand and led her down the corridor, whispering that she'd have to tiptoe so as not to disturb the other staff on their floor. She knew Parminder was in one of the rooms near theirs.

In less than five minutes he was flicking the lights on in the library on the ground floor.

Sadie blinked. The fire in the marble fireplace with its raised slate hearth was crackling. The gardens, which flooded the place with sunlight during the day, were opal-black outside the tall, narrow windows. Without the daytime backdrop, the floor-to-ceiling bookshelves made her feel as if she was back in the seventeenth century.

Owen led her to a soft green couch, motioned for her to sit, and picked up a remote control. Sadie gasped in delight as a huge white screen appeared from the ceiling and a projector high above her head shone the opening titles of Conall McCaskill's movie *Surrender* straight into her eyeline.

'How did you…?'

'I got Fergal to pull a few strings,' he said, and shot her a wink. 'Told him I needed a peace offering.'

He dropped to the couch beside her and reached for a bag he'd obviously left there earlier. So this was what he'd been doing so late… setting this up!

Producing two wine glasses and a bottle of her favourite Chardonnay, he proceeded to apologise.

She interrupted him. 'Let's forget about it.'

'Deal,' he said with a relieved sigh, pressing 'play' on the movie and scooting to the other end of the couch. She swallowed back a strange disappointment at the distance between them, and studied the lines of his handsome profile in the low light. DC Shawn flashed onto the giant screen. It was the famous scene where the character reeled off a list of curses in French, and it sent Owen's expression to new levels of amusement.

'Check Conall out—he looks so young. You know, I got those tests back tonight... Did I tell you I think his depression is linked to reduced activity in the left frontal lobe? Do you think he still knows any French? We should test him... add some language-related exercises into his programme.'

Sadie couldn't talk about Conall McCaskill's linguistic abilities right now. Reaching for the remote, she paused the movie. Crossing her legs towards Owen on the couch, she studied his face.

'You were right, Owen. What you said about Callum.'

Owen sucked in a breath through his nose and shook his head. Suddenly her heartbeat was loud in her ears.

'Sadie, it's none of my business.'

His face was deadly serious in the firelight, and she gripped her wine glass harder, so as not to lean across and wipe away the tiny black smear of what was probably coal dust across his left cheek.

'I made it your business when I cried on you over him,' she said tightly. 'I came to you because we always have fun. Because I knew my tears wouldn't last long with you around.'

Why was her heart doing that weird fluttery thing again?

'But you were right, Owen. He didn't exactly set my heart on fire. And I'm going to make better choices from now on.'

'Well, don't look to me as a role model,' he shot back, but his eyes narrowed as he searched hers, as if he was wrestling with a need to eject some further self-deprecation. She knew he always cracked jokes when he was nervous.

Owen took their glasses away and scooted a little closer. He reached for her with his big, familiar warm hands and held hers lightly, turning her wrists this way and that contemplatively as he spoke.

'I know I push people away when they get too close. But I'm not... I don't want to...'

'What *do* you want, Owen?'

Sadie felt her breath catch. She forced herself to meet his eyes, even though suddenly it felt like a loaded question that involved her and caused the blood to throb in her veins. What exactly was she wanting him to say, here?

'What I want is...' Owen faltered and went quiet, still turning her hands over in his.

The fire spat and hissed. A cat screeched somewhere outside. The moment felt eternal. A memory flickered to the forefront of her brain and fizzled out before she could catch it. Was it the memory of a moment when they'd been like this before? Close… On a precipice…

She found herself leaning into him slowly, studying the slight stubble across his jawline, then looking back up to his eyes. The gap between their faces grew smaller and smaller. For just a second she honestly thought they were going to…

Owen closed his eyes an inch from her face and dashed both hands through his hair. The moment evaporated. *Poof.* Gone.

'What I really want is popcorn,' he announced, unfurling himself from the cushions with the speed of a cheetah and making for the door. 'I left it in my room. I'll be right back.'

Sadie pressed her palms to her eyes. Her cheeks felt clammy and her toes were numb from sitting cross-legged, frozen in place, waiting… waiting…waiting for what?

Oh. My. God.

What the heck had just happened? Had they almost *kissed*?

Making a steeple of her still-warm fingers, she closed her eyes and caught her breath. That had been a lucky escape. He could have kissed her right then, and she could've kissed him back, and that would've ruined everything! Owen was the only stable thing in her life. Rocking this boat they were on was out of the question. Just because he'd done something nice for her…like a boyfriend would.

You must be out of your mind.

She raked her hands through her hair. Portia had got to her, she reminded herself. He might have been about to bop her on the nose or something equally playful. He would *never* try and kiss her. If Owen felt anything remotely romantic towards her it would have happened years ago, and nothing ever *had* happened. She'd never have let it—not with his reputation.

But, then again, she'd never seen him look at her like that before.

And he hadn't actually been with a woman in ages, if what he'd said about America was true. It was almost as if he'd come back from Boston a different person.

Maybe…

No. She hugged her knees to her chest against the cushions. Owen was off-limits. He'd never give her the commitment, the wedding, the children… He hated all that stuff. All the stuff she wanted. And even if he did decide to want it, who was to say he wouldn't change his mind? Then she'd lose her best friend for ever.

Will you just calm down?

Fanning herself and soothing her hammering heart with long, deep breaths, she settled into a corner of the couch and did not move—even when he returned with the popcorn and joined her in their silent agreement to act as if nothing had happened.

CHAPTER SIX

'WHAT AN ABSOLUTE BUTE,' Owen quipped, sweeping his arm out over the windswept ocean.

Sadie smirked and huddled further into her coat, which she'd already mumbled about not being quite warm enough. The beach at Ettrick Bay stretched a mile ahead of them, and if he tried hard enough he could *still* picture Thailand.

He went to take his coat off, then paused. Would it be too weird to offer Sadie his jacket after what had happened a few nights ago? The thing they still hadn't talked about.

'*Oui, s'il vous plaît, j'aimerais votre veste,*' she said now in French, which she was pretty good at.

They'd been encouraging Conall McCaskill to remember his French all morning. Sadie's mouth twitched with another smirk below another pair of oversized sunglasses as she held her hand out expectantly.

Shuffling out of his jacket, he settled on handing it over, rather than attempting to do the gentlemanly thing and draping it over her shoulders. For a moment, as she slid her arms into the well-worn leather sleeves and was instantly swamped, the tension that had been there all morning, and for the last few days, lifted.

'Do you think he's making any progress?' she asked him, nodding towards Conall McCaskill. He was squatting on the sand, looking content for maybe the first time ever, tearing bits of bread from a loaf to feed a flock of birds.

'I think so. I think he secretly loves saying lines from *Surrender* in French,' he replied. 'Especially the curse words.'

Thanks to his success in identifying the decreased activity in the actor's left frontal lobe as an antagonist for his ongoing depression, Owen had assigned him a number of rehabilitation exercises to target that area of the brain specifically. Unfortunately, frontal lobe damage often affected an individual's motivation to participate in goal-directed behaviours, like rehabilitation itself, so they hadn't told Conall what they were doing, specifically.

They were being sneaky, but successfully remembering parts of his old screenplay in French whilst casually taking in the sights seemed to be cheering him up.

To their shock, Conall strode over to a dog-walker, who'd stopped to stare in disbelief. He even crouched down to pose for a photo with her huge brown Labrador. Sadie chuckled and shot Owen a look—and *boom!* He was straight back on that couch the other night, closer than close, seconds away from kissing her, and forcing himself not to.

'You talk to him more than I do,' he said to her, clearing his throat, focusing on Conall. 'At least you seem to be getting to him with whatever it is you talk about in your sessions. He only agrees on outings if you come along too.'

'He mentioned his son to me yesterday, actually,' she said, hugging his jacket around her more tightly. 'It was the first time he's brought him up.'

'What did he say?'

'He didn't say much about the accident,' she said, thoughtfully. 'He just talked about the first time Scott said he wanted to be a stuntman. Somehow the kid got up on the roof in a Superman cape and tried to fly off it. He was only five years old. Wound up in hospital with a broken arm.'

'Ouch.' Owen sucked in a breath. 'Who could've predicted his stunts would actually kill him all these years later?'

Sadie looked at him sideways. 'Conall's lost a part of his soul, Owen. Everything is meaningless to him now, which is why he's so angry and cold. I saw myself in him the whole time he was speaking, because it was how *I* felt after Chris died.'

Her chin wobbled slightly, and then she bowed her head. Suddenly Sadie had that look his mum had always used to have when she was trying to stop another tidal wave of emotion from sweeping her away. A stone formed in his stomach.

'Did you talk about Chris to Conall?' he asked now, remembering she hardly ever talked about her brother—not to anyone.

She nodded, biting down on her lip.

'You can talk to me about him if you ever need to,' he heard himself say, reaching for her hand amongst the folds of his jacket.

Why had he never said that before?

'Thank you,' she whispered, squeezing his fingers only slightly before dropping them. 'But this isn't about me.'

They stood together, watching their patient, and he wrestled with the questions he'd never felt permitted to ask her before.

'What happened that made you never want to talk about it?' he ventured eventually, deciding now was as good a time as any. 'If you want to tell me now, I mean. No pressure.'

'Nothing,' she said quickly. 'People die, Owen, and it's horrible, and gut-wrenching, and a million things you can't describe. But that's just a part of it. After that there's nothing. That's the worst. When you can't even think of a reason to breathe.'

Sadie wrapped her arms around herself again and a chill seized his bones, rooting him to the spot. Death's shadow hadn't fallen on him yet. At least, it hadn't taken anyone close to him. He'd always assumed he'd deal with it just fine. Everyone died, like she said, but it was a part of life; it shouldn't necessarily stop you living yours.

But something about her face had him holding his breath. He'd just put up walls...so as not to feel anything. Maybe that was why he'd never pressed Sadie on the details of her brother's death. Deep down he couldn't face what was coming for him. One day that pain would become his, with his mum, even his dad, for all his sins. And, sure, things weren't perfect, but he wasn't ready for *that*. Not by a long shot.

'It took me a long time to get myself out of that and deal with both my parents...'

'They divorced right after he died, didn't they?'

'Not right after. It was more like a slow unravelling. It eventually happened during my first year at Imperial—before we'd even met.'

'But it's not like you never speak to them,' he said.

He'd heard her on the phone with them, separately, a few times.

'I speak to them. But it's never about anything

real. They don't talk about Chris…or what was wrong with him. Seventeen-year-old guys don't just decide to die unless there's something really wrong, Owen. He was my younger brother and we were close. I should've noticed it sooner. My parents…' She trailed off, closing her mouth firmly.

'He *killed* himself?'

Owen's heart was skidding under his shirt. How had he never known this? He'd always assumed it had been a terrible accident.

'He said he couldn't "do life" any more,' Sadie said. 'I found the note. He stuck it on the inside of his bedroom door, right before he took his motorbike out. I think he fell in with the wrong crowd…drugs, maybe. He'd started getting moody and secretive…but before that he was the happiest, most laid-back kid you'd ever met.'

'Holy hell…'

Pulling himself together, Owen took her shoulders gently, forcing her to face him, tilting her chin up.

What the hell? I should've known this sooner.

But she'd never said any of this before.

'I'm so sorry you went through all that, but surely you don't blame yourself in any way, do you, Sadie? Your parents don't blame you for what happened?'

'I don't want to think about it, Owen,' she said, avoiding his eyes. 'Your friendship means so much to me. You help me more than you know, even when we don't talk about all that stuff.'

Owen flinched inside at the way she emphasised the word friendship—like a reminder to him not to get too close.

'You wouldn't be you if that "stuff" hadn't happened,' he said. 'And for the record you can *always* talk to me—about whatever you like.'

He almost added something like *That's what friends are for*, but he refrained. He wasn't much of a friend if he hadn't even known all this till now. He'd been too wrapped up in his own family sagas to notice she'd had one of her own—something way, way worse.

'I'm so sorry I never knew about any of this,' he said.

'Why would you? I never told you.'

Dropping his hands from her shoulders, he wrestled with a sudden urge to pull her closer, but he knew nothing would suffice in this moment.

The wind whipped up her hair and the seagulls swooped around them and he couldn't get her words out of his head. How could he not have known? And what else had he totally missed about Sadie? If she blamed herself in any way for not seeing suicide speeding up on her brother—or, worse, if her parents blamed her for not being an attentive enough sister… Well, that was a hell of a lot more than he knew what to do with right now. It needed some serious processing.

'Did you want to kiss me the other night?' she asked him suddenly, out of nowhere.

What?

Sadie was scanning his eyes. He was still reeling from the news about her brother's suicide and now she was bringing this up?

'Because you *have* to be thinking about it, too. It was a bit of a weird moment between us, right? On the couch…before you went to get the popcorn?'

Owen's stomach tied itself into one huge knot as he grappled with how to answer. Her gaze was loaded. He'd assumed they'd both decided to forget it, but here they were. She'd clearly been thinking about it as much as he had.

Before he could stop himself he launched into an award-winning American accent. 'You're pretty as a picture, but you're the last person I'd want to kiss, Sadie Mills.'

Sadie just nodded thoughtfully and was silent for longer than was comfortable. Then she said a very quiet 'Good…' and he kicked himself as she pulled out her phone, signalling the end of their discussion.

Great job, Owen. Way to ruin a serious conversation.

'Hey, you two. *J'ai besoin d'une tasse de café!*' Conall McCaskill was done with feeding the birds and was strolling purposefully towards them, shouting something about coffee?

'Sure, we'll swing by the tearoom,' Sadie chirped, and then she said it again in French, stepping away from Owen and motioning them all down the beach.

Owen's jaw ticked as he followed after them, watching her in his jacket.

You're the last person I'd want to kiss, Sadie Mills…

Why the hell had he said that—and in such a stupid way, too? Right after she'd dropped the bombshell about her brother.

Sadie knew him. She knew he used humour whenever he felt cornered, or when he wanted to distance himself from something…or someone. He'd said she could always talk to him, and then he'd shown her she actually couldn't.

Idiot.

In the quaint, aquatic-themed white and blue tearoom, Conall wore sunglasses—which, of course, meant more people recognised him than ever. Word was already out that he was staying in the small town, but when Sadie asked if he'd rather leave and go back to Rothesay he was firm in his decision.

'Non, merci.'

Outings like this were imperative when it came to Sadie monitoring his progress in society.

And Owen took this new attitude as a sign that the actor was feeling better about being around people than before—thanks to the confidence boost whenever a forgotten word or phrase came back to him, and of course Sadie's constant efforts to coax his grief out into the open, instead of smothering it with rage and alcohol.

His thoughts kept slipping from analysing Conall's movements to Sadie. What she must have gone through, losing her brother to suicide. She'd learned her skills from her own experience as much as from her studies—what to do and what *not* to do when a person's grief overcame them in her presence. He'd pretty much made a habit out of making life a joke around her since they'd met, so it was no wonder she hadn't ever opened up to him properly about the things that actually mattered to her.

But then on his end there had always been an underlying fear of letting her get too close, he supposed. Just in case those feelings ever came back.

Showing his true emotions had brought him nothing but disdain from his mother while he was growing up, and he wasn't very good at showing them now. Not that getting yelled at for being a sniffling and 'useless' person when he was eleven was an excuse any more. That had been years ago!

'Is it OK to get a photo?' A young mother approached, wanting a selfie with Conall.

'No charge for you,' Conall told her, sliding out of his chair and causing the rest of the people in the café to turn and stare.

Owen moved his chair to make more room, and both his arm and knee made contact with Sadie's. She shot him a sideways glance and immediately the tension was back.

Undeniable.

It practically filled the busy bustling tearoom.

She shifted her chair around too, so they weren't touching, and Owen found his foot tapping impatiently under the table. Was it going to be weird between them now?

'We'll have to go if this continues,' she told him, bobbing her head towards the photo session.

For a second he thought she meant if this weirdness between them continued, and he was about to agree. But…

'I know this was his idea,' she went on'. 'But we're not supposed to be encouraging people to—'

'I know when you two are talking about me,' Conall interrupted, as the woman moved off with her daughter. 'I decide what I do with my fans, and when.'

Their surly star was back, grumpy as ever.

Conall slipped on his jacket while someone

else sneaked a photo of him from behind. 'But you're right—we should get going.'

Owen went to hand Sadie his jacket again. It was still pretty chilly outside. But this time she refused.

They spent the ride back in their private car in silence. Both Sadie and Conall stared out of the window from the back seat, seemingly lost in thought. Owen ground his teeth in the passenger seat.

It *was* awkward now. Even if Conall hadn't been in the car it would have been awkward. Confusion spun into irritation. Did she honestly think he would have kissed her that night?

OK, yes, maybe he'd been thinking about it, in another momentary lapse of judgement, but he'd never actually *do* it. That would just be messy. Sadie needed someone who could give her all the things he couldn't offer anyone right now—maybe not ever. Who could blame her after what she'd been through?

He was just contemplating how he could continue to be there for her as a friend, and thinking how much that actually sucked, when Sadie's phone chirped loudly in her pocket. Her face fell as she answered the call.

'What is it?' he asked, instincts primed.

'It's Portia,' she told him, one hand over the phone. 'Driver, please hurry—we need to get back!'

CHAPTER SEVEN

THEY FOUND PORTIA flat on her back in the yoga studio. Dr Calhoun was on her knees, one hand on Portia's clammy forehead, trying to force the poor woman to keep the oxygen flowing. The harrowing howls coming from Portia vibrated in Sadie's ears.

'It started with the usual tingle and escalated faster than usual,' Dr Calhoun explained as Sadie and Owen knelt at her side.

'You were doing so well on the new programme,' Sadie said to Portia as Owen took over with the oxygen. 'It's just a setback. It has made a difference, I promise.'

'I know, but I could feel this coming on when I woke up.' She winced. 'Ooh, I miss Stan... I need my husband.'

'We'll call him soon,' she promised.

The other in-patients were hovering outside the studio, dressed in their activewear. They'd been midway through a blissful yoga-nidra class, apparently, when Portia's cluster headache had caught up with her.

'You can leave me with Owen and Sadie,' Portia managed to tell Dr Calhoun, clutching Owen's wrist as he tried to adjust her mask. 'They know what to do.'

Portia drew a few more sharp consecutive breaths from the apparatus as Dr Calhoun closed the door after her, but her eyes were streaming like waterfalls and Sadie could only imagine the searing red-hot agony she must be experiencing around her skull.

Suicide headaches. That was what they called them.

The name usually sent her mind in a thousand directions, but today she pushed all thoughts of Chris away. It had been bad enough seeing Owen looking at her with pity just now, after what she'd told him. Ever since he'd been looking at her differently, and it made her deeply uncomfortable—especially as she'd brought up their almost-kiss, too.

Well, she couldn't have ignored the giant elephant in the room much longer, even if *he'd* wanted to.

She helped him now, getting Portia to her knees instead of lying on her back.

'Deep breaths from your belly, not your mouth, remember,' he told her. 'Concentrate. Distract your mind. It can only focus on one thing at a time...'

Sadie held Portia's hand, wishing that were true, while Portia did everything Owen asked and had probably instructed her to do before, in case this ever happened.

The yoga studio was small, white and bright. Various ferns in crocheted hanging baskets made living drapes over the floor-to-ceiling windows, and six purple yoga mats sat ominously empty nearby on the hardwood floor. Not a place for this much pain, Sadie observed grimly.

'That's right...in and out...deep and deeper,' Owen instructed—right before Portia emitted another yowl that tore Sadie's heart into shreds.

She squeezed Portia's hand tighter and reminded her that this would pass. Even though the cruel attack seemed to last for ever.

'I ate a bacon sandwich,' Portia told them eventually, squeezing her eyes shut as if it hurt to speak.

Owen's brow crinkled in confusion.

'It's the only thing I ate that was different,' the woman explained after a moment, courageously swallowing back another stab of pain.

'She's been keeping a journal,' Sadie explained.

'Oh, yes,' Owen replied, without meeting her eyes. 'So it's nitrates...the nitrates in bacon that's one of the triggers. Good to know.'

'It's always the things I love most that cause this,' Portia said next, still wincing although the deep breaths and oxygen finally seemed to be helping somewhat. 'It used to happen after I had sex with my husband. I'm sure he thought I was possessed. He refused to make love to me for months—can you believe it?'

'Well, if sex caused you this much pain, I can,' Sadie replied thoughtfully, imagining for a moment being possessed, her legs locked around some equally wicked demon lover, begging for more. Owen's face flashed onto the image and she swallowed it away.

What?

'We'll get your sex-life back on track, don't worry,' Owen announced.

'Promises, promises,' Portia responded. Her headache was seemingly abating with every breath. 'It's not every day someone like you tells me something like that, Dr Penner.'

'Good to see you've got your sense of humour back,' Sadie interjected, helping her sit up as a stab of something like jealousy surprised her.

The forty-eight-year-old woman was decidedly less pale now, and it hadn't escaped Sadie's attention that she was very attractive for her age. Hmm… Maybe telling Portia about her and Owen's past had ignited Portia's imagination. Maybe she was conjuring up all sorts of thoughts about

Owen in the confines of her room, Sadie thought. She was missing her husband, after all.

Irritation tingled around her nerves as Owen waggled his eyebrows in her direction. He was clearly humouring Portia she was their patient after all.

When Portia announced that she was feeling much better they helped her out of the studio together, supporting her on each side, and took her back to her suite. Sadie stood outside the bathroom while Portia changed out of her yoga clothes, and felt Owen lasering her back with his eyes.

Every time he addressed her about anything at all, she regretted asking if he'd wanted to kiss her. But if she hadn't it would have made things even *more* awkward. He must be thinking about it too—how could he not be?

Asking him about it had been a good way of trying to distract him from asking any more questions about Chris or her estranged family, she supposed. That topic always brought up way too many emotions. More than she had the time or energy to deal with—especially with patients around.

Conall McCaskill was in her head *and* in her heart already. All that pain in his eyes... All she'd seen in the way he'd wrung his hands on his lap when he'd talked about Scott in their last session... It had touched her, and dragged her through Chris's death all over again. It was to be expected, always. It was part of her job. But this time Owen had seen it.

She had no place for vulnerability. It would only set her back on this path she'd forged for herself since all that.

They closed the door on Portia's suite, leaving her to rest, and walked down the photo-lined corridor. Sunlight streamed in through the windows onto Owen's face as they made small talk about how Portia's diet would need even closer monitoring, with the help of Saskia, the resident nutritionist.

Sadie had one foot on the stairs when Owen took her arm and pulled her back up to the landing. Her heart skyrocketed right up to the turrets as he searched her eyes.

'Sadie, how are you?'

'What? I'm fine…'

'I've been thinking about what you told me earlier…about Chris.'

Oh, God.

He paused, and something about his hand on the sleeve of her jumper made sweat break out on the back of her neck.

'Listen, if you ever need to—'

'I don't. I told you,' she said quickly, hating the look of sympathy on his face. Fresh annoyance at herself made her cheeks sting as she removed herself from his concerned grip. 'I shouldn't have told you the details. You didn't need to know.'

Owen stepped back from her, looking slightly wounded. 'I'm just sorry I never asked you about it before.' He lowered his voice, his obvious concern for her making his eyes crease. 'He committed *suicide*, Sadie...that's a little different from dying in a motorcycle accident. You do know that's what I thought happened, all this time?'

'Why wouldn't you have thought that?' she said staunchly. 'I didn't elaborate on the details.'

'I know—but why not?'

Sadie shrugged, wishing her stomach would stop tangling itself into that giant knot. This was exactly what she didn't want to happen. Her best friend looking at her as if she needed to be swaddled in cotton wool, or as if she had some problem he now had to fix, like everyone else in here. It was bad enough that she hadn't seen it coming with Chris. The last thing she wanted was for Owen to start poking around.

'It happened a long time ago, Owen. I'm fine,' she said stiffly, adjusting her wristwatch.

'But you're not, are you? And Conall's getting to you, bringing it all up whenever he talks about losing Scott...'

'It's my job, Owen. And I'll deal with it like I always do. Without your help.'

Owen straightened his shoulders and blew air from his nose, and she knew she wouldn't escape this confrontation. She'd told him something deeply personal and made it his business—like she always seemed to do with Owen lately, despite trying not to.

'I have to go to my next appointment,' she said, hurrying on down the stairs ahead of him.

'Of course you do,' he muttered behind her.

Great—now she'd offended him. And she knew that was grossly unfair. But it was better than feeling torn by his lips being too close again, his eyes being too probing again.

What was she meant to do with all this? It was bad enough that she was even having these weird new feelings for her friend. And he felt the same, she could tell. When he'd said he'd never kiss her this morning…that had been a *blatant* lie. He always did one of those stupid accents whenever he felt put on the spot.

But Owen Penner never wanted more than a good time, and she was not about to let him make *her* his next good time—not for anything.

Sadie continued with her appointments and somehow managed to eat her dinner in the little courtyard outside without Owen interrupting her, like he usually did. As the sun set that evening she still hadn't seen him again.

Good, she thought. For both of them.

She needed to stop treating him like one of her 'comfort blankets' just because there was no one else around who knew her. She'd already decided there would be no more comfort blankets, and here she was, spilling all her issues out to Owen!

That would get her nothing apart from his quick rejection—like he rejected anyone who got too close to him.

Something woke her at three a.m. Sadie shot up in bed, fresh from a fitful dream about Chris calling out to her from somewhere she couldn't reach. Awful!

Pulling on her white embroidered robe and slippers, she made her way downstairs. Sleep would be impossible now, so she might as well make a cup of tea and get some fresh air.

The spring night was unusually mild and welcoming outside. Sadie found herself strolling by the fernery, breathing in the sweet scent of the jasmine trees that lined its entrance, recalling bits of her dream. Just talking about her parents and Chris so briefly to Owen had brought everything back. No wonder it was creeping into her dreams.

Everything was haunting her now—the fact that she hadn't seen just how much Chris had needed help. The fact that guilt had kept her away from home for so long…long enough that she hadn't even known her parents were getting a divorce until after it had happened. She'd been the worst sister and the worst daughter.

Her stomach knotted again as she sat by the

silent mermaid fountain, thinking of Owen, too. He'd looked so hurt that she'd never told him the truth about her brother. All this time she'd let him believe what had happened to him was an accident. All this time. And now he probably thought she didn't trust him with anything serious. That all they had were their laughs, their jokes, their good times.

But it was getting harder not to trust him with *more*...she realised. He was always there for her. He would always be there for her.

As a *friend*, she reminded herself, as soon as her heart started its involuntary fluttering again. All this wandering outside the lines had to stop.

Being in love is a waste of time.

He'd said it himself, the day his mum had called. It wasn't something he was looking for right now—maybe ever. He'd probably stay single till he reached his fifties and wanted companionship—and if he did, so what? Why should that be *her* problem? Why was she even still *thinking* about all this? Their friendship was too good to risk for anything!

With a sigh at the moon, she decided that maybe it was time to go back inside.

Nearing her room, she heard a whisper in the corridor that made her start. She tiptoed to the end of a towering oak bookcase and peered around a row of old encyclopaedic volumes to see someone standing outside Owen's door.

A barefooted Owen was propped up in the doorway on one muscled arm, his broad naked chest on full display, and wearing a pair of comfy checked pyjama bottoms. Pressing her back to the wall and huddling into her robe, she tried to make out what was going on, but she couldn't hear a thing...except soft laughter between a man and a woman.

At four a.m.?

Hunched in the shadow of the bookcase, Sadie tried her best to slow the sudden pounding of her suspicious heart. Eventually Owen closed his door, with one last soft, telling chuckle. His visitor walked straight past her, oblivious, and Sadie dared a peek just as whoever it was unlocked a nearby door and slipped inside.

Even from the back, the woman's long, black satiny hair and dark exotic grace was a giveaway.

Sadie stood there, fuming in the darkness.

Parminder.

Owen was meeting Parminder in the middle of the night.

CHAPTER EIGHT

OWEN CARVED INTO a slice of the chicken on his plate, tracking the busy dining room for Sadie. She hadn't stepped foot in here at the usual time for the last five days, and he had a feeling she was afraid he'd probe her about her past again. As if he'd dare!

If she'd wanted to talk about the grief and the guilt she still carried around she would have told him the full story before now, but obviously she didn't trust him with the serious stuff. He was the joker. The stand-in comfort blanket till she found someone more suitable to handle her heart. The *pleasure-seeker*.

'Penny for your thoughts!'

A voice broke into his depressing internal monologue.

'What?'

'You look like you're thinking about something very serious. And you're murdering your peas.'

Parminder slid in next to him, and he realised

he'd turned his green peas into tiny explosions, smashed on his plate. He also noticed she'd undone the top three buttons of her shirt, revealing just a hint of cleavage—for his benefit, no doubt.

Parminder had been finding new reasons to talk to him for days—ever since she'd knocked on his door in the middle of the night several days ago in a skimpy nightdress, claiming to be scared after seeing a ghost. It was in his best interests to be polite to her right now, but he'd have preferred to eat in peace or with Sadie.

Where was she, anyway? Avoiding his probing was one thing, taking it to extremes by missing the famous Rothesay Recovery Sunday lunch was not like her at all.

Parminder started telling him about Conall McCaskill's latest spat with a doctor. 'He was only doing a regular check-up, but Mr McCaskill almost got violent. Apparently he only wants to deal with you and Dr Mills going forward.'

Owen frowned at his potatoes. Conall's recent setback was the talk of Rothesay this morning, and it was very disheartening to say the least. He still wouldn't talk about Scott's accident with him, but all healing was a work in progress, after all.

'Might be time to help redirect that anger into something more aggressive than potting plants... like woodwork, or bag punching...' Parminder was still offering advice on Conall, and he forced himself to pay attention.

'Maybe he could learn to play the bagpipes,' he offered. 'Those guys always look like their lungs are about to burst. Could be a good way to tire him out. I'll talk to Sadie about it.'

Speak of the devil.

In walked Sadie—finally. His back tensed all over again as their eyes met.

'Would you mind?' he asked Parminder quickly, and reluctantly she shuffled over and made room for Sadie next to him at the table.

'I knew you wouldn't miss the roast lunch,' he said as Sadie slid into the seat, eyeing him cautiously. Her potatoes were drowning in gravy, as usual. 'Is there chicken under there somewhere too?' he joked, trying to lift the immediate tension between them.

'I like gravy,' she said simply, reaching across him for the pepper.

He caught her arm softly and leaned closer, away from Parminder's hearing. 'Are you OK? You've been…noticeably absent.'

'I've been busy,' she replied curtly, removing her arm and shifting her eyes to Parminder. 'I'm sure you have been too.'

He frowned at her. She knew his schedule the same way he knew hers. She hadn't been *that* busy.

'What were you two talking about just now?' Sadie asked casually.

The way she'd pulled her hair back tight and buttoned her blouse three times higher than Parminder's, right to her throat, made her look like a strict headmistress.

'Parminder and I were discussing how Mr Mc-Caskill should play the bagpipes,' he said, thinking how hot she looked, all prim and proper. 'Maybe we can add it to his rehab regimen, to help him get some anger out.'

Sadie huffed a laugh. 'Just because he's Scottish it doesn't mean he automatically wants to know how to play the bagpipes, Owen. Besides, bagpipes make people angry.'

He chuckled. 'You have a point. But I've come here to Scotland. I want bagpipes.'

A smile teetered on her lips, but it vanished as Parminder cut in enthusiastically.

'Maybe *you* should learn, Owen?' She tossed her veil of long black hair over her shoulder and almost knocked a spoon off the table, too. 'We'll get you a kilt too. I bet you'd look good in one.'

'Now, that I wouldn't mind,' he mused, imagining it for a moment. 'I've heard the fresh Scottish air feels damn fine blowing in under a kilt…'

Sadie stood up again quickly, taking her plate with her. 'I've left my book upstairs. I'll eat in my room.'

Parminder stopped her giggling abruptly and scraped her chair back, looking at Sadie in horror. 'You're not going upstairs on your own, are you?'

Sadie paused. 'What do you mean?'

'Well, aren't you scared you might see the ghost?'

'I don't believe in ghosts.'

'Parminder's eyes grew wide and beseeching. With a lowered voice she said, 'I saw it…*her*. The other night. Ask Owen. I saw the Lady in White.'

Owen pulled a face. How was he supposed to know what she'd seen? He'd been fast asleep till she'd pounded on his door. 'All I know is that you were scared enough by something to wake me at some ungodly hour,' he said.

Slowly, Sadie lowered herself into the chair again, turning to Parminder. 'You saw the Lady in White?'

Parminder bobbed her head, her eyes darting around the room. 'I got up for a wee and I saw her walking in the garden…all around the fernery and the fountain. But she could be anywhere, right? I haven't been anywhere on my own in this place all week.'

Sadie just stared at her plate. A small smile crept over her face before she picked up her cutlery and resumed eating without a word.

'I know you don't believe me,' Parminder continued, glancing vexedly at her.

'I believe you saw *something*,' Sadie said carefully.

Her eyes flashed to his, and for just a second he saw the old Sadie…the Sadie he'd missed since things had started getting weird. Maybe things *could* go back to normal between them, he thought, wondering all of a sudden what her secret was.

Later that afternoon, Sadie caught him just as he was about to start his regular session with Conall McCaskill.

'Apparently he's asked for both of us today,' she said, smoothing down her shirt and skirt as they took the corridor towards the actor's suite.

'Parminder told me he only wants to deal with us from now on,' he admitted.

Sadie stopped abruptly, arms folded. She had that look on her face, as if she was about to own up to something.

'About Parminder… You know, I've been so annoyed with you for hooking up with a staff member. I thought you were sleeping with her.'

'Why did you think that?' he asked, mimicking her stance while he processed this new information.

So was that why she'd been so cold with him recently? It wasn't just because he'd overstepped some mark and dredged up deep-rooted insecurities she hated to admit to, even to him… it was because she'd deemed him an unprofessional playboy and didn't want to be associated with his behaviour.

Neither was good.

Unless…she'd been *jealous*?

He studied her intently as she spoke, running the possibilities around in his head, noting with some element of concern that he rather enjoyed the thought that she'd been jealous.

'I saw her the other night, after she'd knocked on your door. I was already awake, and coming back to my room. I think it was me she saw down by the fernery, Owen. I was wearing my white robe!'

'The ghost of Sadie walks the grounds at night, tricking the staff?' He smirked.

Sadie pretended to thump him. 'Don't tell her. Then I'd have to admit I saw her that night at your door but didn't say anything, and she'll think I'm weird.'

'You *are* weird,' he confirmed, and she pulled a face at him that made him laugh. 'You didn't tell *me* what you saw, though. That's not like you. Usually I'd get an earful about something like that. Were you jealous?'

'Well, obviously this place is not haunted,' she said thoughtfully, without answering his question. 'Even though there are still those weird banging noises at night. Have you heard them lately?'

'No, but at least now you know it's not *me* who's been doing the banging,' he replied, watching her fiddle with her shirtsleeve buttons, seeing the way she was biting on her lip, the fresh blush of colour on her cheeks. 'For the record, Parminder's crush is all one-sided,' he told her seriously.

'Well, that's good to know,' she replied, talking to the floor. 'Because it wouldn't be very professional to start something up while we're... while you're here.'

'Noted,' he said with a salute, refusing to mention her fumbled Freudian slip as she led the way into Conall McCaskill's suite.

That look. He'd know it a mile off. Women always had that lips pursed, eyes narrowed look when they were jealous. God, if only he could act on his sudden burning urge to grab her, throw her over his shoulder and carry her up to his room. And then throw her on his bed and show her just what her jealousy did to him.

Luckily the A-lister was in a better mood today, but they still had to discuss his recent violent outburst with the other doctor.

'He mentioned Maeve...how I'm upsetting her because I refuse to subject her to this ridiculous gala event, but what did he expect?' he huffed, stretching out on the couch like a cat. 'What if I don't want to attend myself? Did anyone even consider that? It's not like I can be "switched on" all the time. I told you—I decide when I see my fans.'

Owen caught Sadie's look and shut his mouth. OK, so the guy had a giant ego, but it wasn't entirely a bad thing—at least he was getting some of his confidence back, largely thanks to their speech and language sessions that were bringing up things he actually enjoyed remembering and forcing his depression aside in small bursts.

But Conall's wife had been on the phone several times asking for him, and the stubborn man was refusing to speak to her a lot of the time. He blamed her for sending him here, for assuming he needed special help. His pride had taken a kick—that was the real issue here.

'It's not about subjecting anyone to your fans…it's not a public event,' Sadie informed him softly. 'They do it every year. It started as an fundraising event to entertain Rothesay's supporters, and now every year it marks another year since the recovery unit became what it is now: a successful space for healing.'

Owen heard Sadie's voice, laced with empathy.

'It's supposed to be a chance to include people's spouses,' she continued. 'Perhaps Maeve would like to feel more involved with your healing process, seeing as she's still going through her own. It won't help that process if you feel like someone is shutting you out.'

Owen braced himself for another verbal tirade, but Conall just fiddled with the buttons on his stylish tweed jacket and scowled at the ceiling.

'I suppose you would know that,' he said eventually.

He went on to explain how it was the processing of his grief that had caused his violent outburst, something Sadie had encouraged with her sessions, although he regretted lashing out at the doctor the way he had.

Owen prepared his upcoming questions for the actor's weekly analysis, wondering exactly how much Sadie had divulged to him about her own loss. Just by relating to Conall she'd got more out of him than anyone. But she'd never thought to burden *him* with the truth before.

That was still bothering him like a mosquito… the fact that she didn't trust him with anything serious. But then, it wasn't as if he'd ever given her reason to. She'd always had boyfriends for that. He wasn't settling down…he wasn't cut out for being anyone's rock. Never had he given anyone any indication that he'd stick around for more than a few weeks, and Sadie knew all that. But…

But just now she'd pretty much confirmed a case of the green-eyed Loch Ness monster. That look on her face!

He shook himself, pulling his attention back from dangerous territory. Sadie was not someone he could afford to go there with—not for anything. They'd never had to rely on one another solely for attention before—that was all this was. Even though he'd missed her like hell in America, and was still figuring out what that meant, exactly.

'I asked for you both today because I know I need to talk about the accident itself, and I don't want to say it twice,' Conall was saying now, wringing his hands on the couch. 'I know I've been a little bit of a…well, a *lot* of a grump. But I just miss my boy so much…'

His voice wobbled suddenly. Sadie reached out to place a gentle hand on his.

'I see it every time I close my eyes,' said Conall. 'There isn't a day that goes by when I don't blame myself…'

'It was not your fault,' Owen said, standing up in a primal urge not to upset *anyone* in the room any further.

'But I could have prevented it. If only I'd been watching more closely. It was *my* damn movie set!'

'That doesn't mean anything. It was an accident. Both Dr Mills and I know that—everyone knows that.'

Sadie was silent for a moment, tapping her nails on the arm of her chair, and he wondered again, now he'd learned about Chris's suicide, why she'd chosen a career that must dredge up so many bad memories. And this must feel very close to home for her: Conall McCaskill playing the blame game with himself.

Conall wore the look of a gladiator about to

step into an arena with a tiger. Owen half expected him to shut down again and refuse their help entirely, but then Sadie let out a sigh from somewhere deep in her soul.

'The hardest thing is finding a place to start. I know that,' she said into the silence. 'Deep inside, you feel like if you start thinking about it you won't be able stop. But somewhere in between, Conall, there is a place where you can learn to live with it. You have to trust that you will get there.'

Owen felt a lump in his throat like a golf ball. And then, just like that, the stoic, moody, grieving Conall McCaskill broke into a thousand pieces. Their favourite actor literally *surrendered* in a way no one would ever have expected. It was like opening a valve...everything came rushing out.

It was nine a.m.

Scott was late.

Conall yelled at him for holding up the shoot.

The props department said everything was OK.

Usually Scott would check things himself too... go for a test run. But they were on the clock, time was ticking...

Conall was annoyed with his son for wasting everyone's time.

And then the car sped out of control, and that

*stupid altercation was his last communication
with Scott...*

Maybe it was witnessing someone so strong
expressing his emotions in a way he himself
had never quite been able to. Maybe it was the
look on Sadie's face. But to his shock, as Conall
wiped a hand across his eyes, Owen found he
was fighting back a kind of tidal wave of emotion the likes of which he'd never felt before.

Some time later he found himself at the end of
the dock, looking over the lake, his eyes on the
bobbing fishing boat. Conall's emotional out-
pouring was still playing on his mind, and his
mother would no doubt add to it shortly.

Three missed calls from her, he noted, shoving
his phone back into his pocket. He should give
her the benefit of the doubt—but then she only
ever bombarded him with calls like this when his
dad had done something to offend her.

'Thinking of going fishing again?'

Sadie had found him. He made room for her
on the wooden jetty beside him.

'Conall has called Maeve and asked her to
come to the gala.'

'Good,' he replied as she sat down and drew
her knees up.

She'd changed into jeans and a short green
linen jacket, and he could smell lavender again.

He swallowed back the now familiar pang he felt at her closeness.

'You left that session as soon as you could,' she said. 'Is he getting to you, too?'

Owen grunted. He'd made an excuse to leave without accepting the cup of tea and signed autograph Conall had offered them, and it hadn't all been to do with his next appointment with Vivek Kumar, nor the missed calls on his phone.

'Seeing someone like that, so famous, being so vulnerable... I don't know,' he admitted, tossing a stick out into the water. 'I guess it got to me, yeah. I was more worried about it all affecting *you*, though,' he added quickly. 'After what you've told me lately.'

Sadie's lips twitched. 'That's sweet,' she replied simply, then leaned back on her elbows, as if she were taking in the sky. 'But why do you think I chose this career, Owen? Hearing people work through their grief gives me strength, even after all this time.'

'You're saying helping them helps you, too, in some way?'

She nodded. 'You don't need to worry about me...really.'

Owen thought he would probably always worry about her now, but he understood about her work.

'Do I need to worry about *you*?' she asked him

after a moment, sitting back up and touching a hand to his arm.

He felt himself tense and dragged a hand through his hair.

'I know you try to keep your emotions out of things, Owen, and that's just how you are, but…'

'You're right.' He bristled at her blunt observation. 'Maybe I've never got my dad's voice out of my head, telling me Penner men don't cry. Stuff like that stays with you, Sadie.'

'Your dad said what?' Sadie's jaw dropped.

He massaged the back of his neck. Why had he just told her that?

Sadie pressed a warm hand to his arm, as if rooting him to the dock, and he wrestled with what to say now that she was waiting for an explanation of some kind. He'd never told anyone about the day that had probably shaped him more than he'd ever admitted. He couldn't avoid it now, though. The words were spilling out of him before he could think to shut up.

He'd been eleven years old, almost deafened by the row going on in the kitchen. His mother had been yelling at his dad.

Penner men are useless—all of you. Useless! Your father was the same, and your grandfather too. I don't know why I thought you'd be any different, Jay…

That was when he'd realised his dad had crossed some unthinkable line and his mother was approaching the end of her tether. He'd been sniffling on the stairs, scared the world was crumbling down around him, when his dad had marched right up to him and boomed, *'Penner men don't cry!'*

It had shocked him to the core. But he'd never cried after that. Not a tear...not a trickle of emotion. Not even after his dad had packed his bags and gone to live with his newest fling. His mum had done enough crying for both of them, anyway, and the last thing he'd wanted was to be useless to her.

Owen paused in his monologue, realising Sadie was staring at him, mouth agape.

'Wow...' she breathed. 'Things are even clearer to me now.'

He felt his eyebrows knit together. 'What do you mean?'

Adrenaline flared in his veins as Sadie's eyes glowed with unexpected affection. Somehow the look on her face riled him up all the more, and he wished he could read her mind. She was probably analysing him...putting him into some box. A guy with daddy issues—*great.*

'It was ages ago. Like I said, I was only eleven,' he reminded her stiffly.

'Like you said, stuff like that stays with you,' she replied, turning him to face her.

She pressed one warm palm to his cheek and stroked her thumb softly to the corner of his mouth. His throat tightened as the lips he knew so well but had never actually tasted hovered tantalisingly close. So close that her breath tickled his nose.

An entire drum kit was going off in his chest now.

For a second longing surged through him, and he braced himself...

Her kiss landed on his forehead, right above his brow. 'You are a special kind of person, Owen,' she said.

Special? Great.

Owen dropped her hand, curling his fists into his sides as her warm smile stretched against his skin. A friendly kiss on the forehead. A compliment on how 'special' he was.

God, Owen, you're an idiot. What else did you expect, anyway?

He pulled away, blew out his cheeks and avoided her eyes, even as heat coursed in his veins. That had been weird.

Resting back on his elbows on the dock, he trained his stare on the water, running over his holiday allowance in his head, feeling his stomach revolt at the pity in her eyes. Humiliation, confusion, the urge to run all made a knot in his insides.

'I have a phone call to make,' he said tightly. The words came out a little more coldly than he'd intended.

Sadie frowned at him. 'What did I do?'

'Nothing,' he said. 'I do have a call to make. And I don't need you to psychoanalyse me.'

'It's a little late for that.' She smirked, getting to her feet.

Owen grunted, not giving her the satisfaction of any acknowledgement. He wanted to confide in her and run from her all at the same time. What the hell was that all about?

As she headed for the house without him, he forced himself to stay put.

CHAPTER NINE

VIVEK KUMAR LOOKED more melancholy than usual when Sadie met him in the music room on the day of the gala. He was staring unseeingly at the piano keys. She closed the door behind her, and crept across the plush red carpet, concerned at his expression. He rested his arms across his portly stomach, then unfolded them, and then folded them again on the piano, frowning at the keys as if he didn't know what to do with them.

'You don't have to do this now,' she said kindly, gesturing to the sheet music on the stand. 'If you're having trouble remembering.'

Vivek was a gifted pianist—at least, he had been before the traumatic head injury that had left a scar inside as large as the one that was displayed on his shaved head, down his neck and across his right shoulder.

He exhaled long and deep through his nose, without looking at her. 'No. I want to,' he said, putting his hands to the keys.

He paused, as if trying to force open some

database in his head that he didn't have the password for. Sadie held her breath, staring out through the floor-length windows at the billowing white marquee now dominating the grounds, ready for this afternoon's event. It seemed like people had been talking about it for weeks but she couldn't seem to get excited about it.

Traumatic brain injuries disturbed the delicate chemistry of the brain so its neurons couldn't function normally. Huge changes to Vivek's thinking and behaviour were still taking everyone by surprise—not least him. Sometimes he remembered how to play. Sometimes he didn't. Owen had told him it might take weeks or even months for his brain to resolve the kind of chemical imbalances that could occur with a TBI.

Owen...

She found herself training her eyes on him as he stepped from the marquee and held up a hand to her from the other side of the window. In seconds he was entering the room.

Sadie let free the breath she was holding, then drew in another one. She couldn't help but note that he looked very handsome in his uniform. More so than usual. He'd caught the sun on his face over the past week or so, often fishing alone after his shifts. Now, halfway into May, it was unusually sunny for Scotland at this time of year.

'Are you going to play for us?' he asked Vivek,

closing the door behind him and putting a folder down on a plush velvet chair.

Sadie felt their shoulders brush momentarily as he moved to her side behind the piano stool, and she tried not to feel the now-familiar sensation of unease at his closeness.

He regretted telling her about his dad the other day—she could tell. As if she could possibly be repulsed by seeing the real, vulnerable Owen behind the tough-guy facade.

The doctor in her was intrigued. His parents' harsh words back then had most definitely left their mark. And his mother was *still* in his ear about his dad. What she'd overheard on the fishing boat, back when they'd first heard about his dad's new engagement, was making more and more sense now.

What was it she'd said? Something like, '*I hope you never treat anyone like this.*' Almost accusingly. Almost as if she expected him to turn out just like his dad.

Owen just put up a wall whenever she'd tried to talk more about it to him, and that was understandable, she supposed. She knew there was nothing worse than people probing her about *her* parents. But the thought of anyone making him feel less than adequate about anything was infuriating. He was one of the kindest people she knew…and if they hadn't been best friends, and if the example of his parents hadn't made him dread the thought of ever being in a relationship himself, she might just consider…

She caught herself.

Nope. There were no 'ifs' with Owen. His friendship was all she needed.

Wasn't it?

'I wanted to play for my wife later.' Vivek cut into her thoughts. 'She's bringing my niece, Ashanti. I wanted it to be a surprise for them,' he said despondently.

Owen put a comforting hand to his shoulder. 'You've already made so much progress, Vivek! We haven't been working on your gaze stabilisation and eye-tracking exercises for long and you already say you're not feeling dizzy or off-balance any more, right? That's a real mark of success. We can't force these things. It's possible the piano may come back to you…give it time.'

Owen shot her a look that said maybe it would, maybe it wouldn't. People were only just beginning to understand the severity of concussion—people who had been injured decades ago were only just starting to see why they'd been thinking or acting a certain way for so long. So many brain injuries went undiagnosed…but so many were diagnosed properly, thanks to doctors like Owen.

He was kind of an amazing person…

The thought caught her off guard, especially

as it came with a sense of longing to be in his vicinity always…to be cared for by him.

'Sorry I'm late, by the way,' he said now. 'Maeve McCaskill has just arrived. There's a bit of a crowd in the marquee already.'

'Ooh, really? She's here?'

Sadie cleared her throat. That might have come out a little too enthusiastically.

Owen's mouth twitched. 'You're not going to ask her to sign your apron, are you?'

'I would if I'd known to bring it with me,' she admitted.

'My wife has all her stuff,' announced Vivek, turning from the piano as if a light had come on in his mind. 'She's always leafing through this one cook-book…'

'Ah, so you remember that.' Owen grinned. 'Do any specific dishes come to mind?'

Vivek's smile faded. He shook his head, which told them he did not without him saying another word.

Sadie assisted Owen with Vivek's memory-strengthening exercises, sometimes watching the crowds gathering outside the window for the gala. It was their last session of the day, and once they were done it would be time to put her best dress on, as well as her best foot forward, for the event everyone had been looking forward to for weeks.

Just a few hours later she was chatting with

Portia and her husband Stan—who was just as fabulous as Portia. Their chemistry was undeniable...

And then Owen approached, with the Mc-Caskills on either side of him, as if he'd been appointed as some kind of celebrity security guard. Sadie tried to keep her squeal confined to her throat as none other than Maeve McCaskill held her hand out.

'I've been looking forward to meeting you,' Maeve said warmly, taking her aside so they could talk in private.

She was the epitome of breezy sophistication. But through her admiration, it hit Sadie...what this woman—a mother—had gone through, and how she'd come out the other side. She felt a rush of empathy that almost brought tears to her eyes.

'I'm so glad you could make it,' she said, sincerely. 'And I'm so very sorry for your loss.'

'I wanted to thank you personally for everything you and Dr Penner have done for my husband,' Maeve replied coolly. 'Conall talks about you very highly.'

'He's come a long way,' Sadie said, noting the jolt in her stomach at hearing the words 'you and Dr Penner'.

Owen was looking at her from where the band was setting up, now. He was dressed in a designer jacket and chinos, holding an orange juice, watching her.

She'd expected another smirk from him over her being starstruck, but he seemed to be appreciating her ocean-green summer dress and her smart hip-length jacket and silver sandals. It was one of her favourite outfits, but she'd never felt so self-conscious under his gaze before.

Ever since he'd opened up to her about his parents she'd found herself thinking even more about that almost-kiss. Their relationship felt more honest now...deeper. She'd even considered lately that perhaps she'd pushed him away all these years by refusing to talk about her own family, and he'd responded by doing the same. Now that they were talking about things—serious things—it was clear they had far more in common than she'd ever realised before.

She *was* psychoanalysing him, in her head. But only because he'd become a hundred times more interesting to her.

And sexy.

How had she failed to notice how sexy he was?

Maybe it had taken coming here to the Western Scottish Highlands, far away from everyone who knew them, for her to see how she'd been blocking out her attraction to him ever since that night in Sylvester's. Because of course nothing had ever happened between them...or would *ever* happen. They'd both kicked down that bridge and set fire to it. Which was good.

Except he looked so damn gorgeous right now,

and she couldn't deny she'd been as jealous as hell over Parminder. God, what would it be like to kiss those lips after all this time…?

Suddenly it occurred to her that Maeve Mc-Caskill was still talking to her…and she was zoning out, thinking about Owen again.

The afternoon stretched into sunset. There were games on the lawn, activities in the fernery, a banquet feast complete with a suckling pig, and now this—an organised boat ride around the lake, led by Owen himself.

He looked like the sexiest of sailors at the helm. He'd loosened his shirt at the neck, and his hair in the breeze was cutely dishevelled. Sadie waved off a bee that was buzzing around her face and took in the scene around her from her seat on the wooden boat. For one glorious afternoon Rothesay Recovery had felt more like a country retreat than a luxury medical facility. She couldn't help a huge surge of pride for her patients over everything they'd achieved so far.

Portia nudged her suddenly, waving off the same bee with her other hand. 'Owen looks like he needs some help up there,' she said, winking at her before burrowing her face lovingly in her husband's shoulder.

They seemed so in love, Sadie mused, remembering how Portia had said they were friends first. Friends who'd had sex as an experiment.

Interesting… I would actually love to try that

with Owen. I wonder if he'd go for it... Why does he have to look so hot right now?

'How long have you been with Owen?' Maeve asked, catching her off-guard. 'I was just thinking how good you two look together. Conall never told me you were—'

'Oh, no, we're not a couple,' Sadie cut in, fixing her eyes on Ashanti, Vivek Kumar's seven-year-old niece, who was asking Owen if she could steer the boat.

Had these women read her mind? But Owen *was* looking at her with interest. He'd probably overheard what Maeve had said. Sadie felt her face flush, and was just about to change the subject when a cry from the front of the boat rendered everyone silent.

'It stung me!'

The little girl was on her feet now, flapping her hands about. A ruckus ensued. Poor Vivek looked dumbstruck as his wife scrambled to reach the child and pull her down to sit on the bench, almost toppling overboard. Then Owen stopped the boat in the middle of the lake just as Sadie launched forward to help. The jerk sent her flying, but Owen caught her in his arms and righted her before she'd even had a chance to catch her breath.

'Thank you,' she gasped, gripping his forearms, stunned for a moment.

Poor Ashanti was shrieking in agony, and the boat was bobbing vigorously now.

'Everyone stay calm,' came Owen's authoritative voice. 'It's just a bee sting.'

Just as he said that, however, the little girl seemed to droop and fold like a piece of paper, straight into Sadie's arms.

'She's passed out!' she cried, horrified, sliding to the floor with her.

Owen made a shield around them with his body and his arms.

'Is she allergic to bee stings?' she heard him ask the Kumars.

'I don't know...' came the reply.

'Sure seems like she is,' someone else responded.

Vivek's eyes grew wide as saucers, but then the girl seemed to regain consciousness, and sucked in a breath as if her life depended on it. She panted a little, her cheeks paling further, and in the middle of the chaos Sadie heard Conall McCaskill step in and offer to take the helm.

With concern, Sadie registered the distance to the jetty. There was no doubt about it—the girl was in the early stages of anaphylactic shock and there was nothing they could do without a shot of epinephrine—which no one had. She and Owen were the only medical staff on the boat.

Owen had called the emergency services already, and was radioing Rothesay Recovery. Everyone was flapping about in a panic now, as she cradled the semi-conscious girl in her arms. Conall McCaskill clambered to the front seat and started steering the boat back the way they'd come. They'd travelled pretty far out from the shore on the huge lake.

Sadie felt Owen's steady hand on her shoulder. 'We've got this,' he whispered to her, causing her ear to tingle. 'She's going to be OK.'

Sadie met Owen's piercing eyes. The fact that he was here gave her comfort, in spite of the situation. She trusted him, and so did everyone else. He had this under control.

Just then a judder from the engine sent them both flailing into each other again. Ashanti gasped as the sound of the motor sputtered into nothing. McCaskill tried to get it going again, tugging with all his might, but he failed and another panicked ruckus broke out amongst the passengers.

Owen was peeling off his shirt.

'What are you doing?' she asked, but Owen already had one foot on the side and in seconds was in the water, gripping the boat from the outside.

'Pass her over to me—we don't have much time,' he said.

'Is he insane?' someone muttered behind her.

But Sadie lowered the young girl into his arms and quickly tore her dress over her head before sliding into the lake too, causing Vivek to gasp and avert his eyes, and Portia to clap her hands approvingly.

Together, she and Owen kept Ashanti's head out of the water as they swam back towards the jetty, every stroke feeling as if they were carving through ice, despite the earlier warmth of the day. The little girl's eyes and lips were swollen, as if the bee had injected its venom straight into her face. Sadie was sure her own face must be blue, and already she could barely feel her fingers and toes, but nothing mattered except getting this girl to safety. Untreated anaphylaxis could lead to death within half an hour.

Parminder met them on the jetty, her bright patterned floral sundress a beacon to swim for. They were all shivering wildly, but Owen made a quick job of lifting the girl to the dock, where Parminder wrapped a blanket around her. Fergal handed Sadie a towel to cover herself—but not before making a full body-swipe with his eyes over her bra and knickers.

An ambulance's siren was already adding its own soundtrack to the air and Owen had started CPR. The scene was surreal, and she was sure the cold would have buckled her knees if she hadn't already been on them on the jetty beside him.

They could have died in that freezing cold lake… A life lived with Owen that ended without so much as a kiss…

Why are you thinking about this now? You're clearly in shock.

Just as two paramedics tore down the path through the garden with a stretcher Ashanti spluttered back to consciousness again, and complained of being cold and dizzy. A rush of relief brought tears to Sadie's eyes as Owen wrapped both of his big arms around her shivering body. She leaned into him, letting the paramedics take over with the epinephrine. Their praise for their quick thinking and heroic action washed over her—all she could think, as she huddled into Owen, was it might have been too late for Ashanti.

It had almost been too late.

'She's going to be OK,' Owen told her, as if he was reading her mind.

His eyes were flooded with concern for her and she wondered if her lips were blue. She let him help her to her feet as the ambulance sped away.

'They'll have to keep her in overnight, in case the symptoms recur, but she's fine—you guys made sure of that,' Parminder said.

Sadie realised people were watching them, standing locked together wrapped in towels and blankets. She pulled away from Owen just as a noise behind them made them all spin around. Sadie blinked. There in the distance was the boat, Conall McCaskill at the helm standing tall, steering towards them at speed, like the action hero he'd once been. Everyone on it was cheering.

'How did you get it to go again?' Sadie said when he pulled up at the jetty, windswept but delighted to learn that Ashanti was fine. He was wearing a look of determination on his handsome face that Sadie hadn't seen since the night they'd re-watched his movie, *Surrender.*

'You don't spend years on movie sets without learning a few things,' he said simply, helping his wife back on to safe, solid ground. A glimmer of pride in his eyes twinkled its way through his tough exterior. Even more so when Maeve flung both arms around him and kissed his cheek, as if she knew she was finally getting her husband back.

'We should go and get changed,' Owen said to her, as someone handed them their clothes from the boat.

Vivek's frantic wife was ushered away by Fergal, to follow the ambulance to the hospital.

The adrenaline was wearing off now, and Sadie was starting to shiver even more. Owen's arm slid around her waist again, and this time she didn't shake him off. She needed him and he knew it.

Her heart thumped wildly, both at what had just happened and his closeness, and their dripping wetness left a watery trail all the way back to the house.

CHAPTER TEN

SADIE STUMBLED HALFWAY up the staircase. Owen caught her, pulling her soaking frame against his bare chest.

'Careful,' he said.

'I'm so cold.' She shivered, as if he might be in doubt. 'How are you not freezing?'

'Adrenaline?'

He met her eyes for a second as she drew long, jagged breaths, and then held her close to steady her as they made their way up the rest of the stairs, trying to ignore the way her skin against his was igniting every cell in his body.

The house was eerily quiet everywhere. Most people were still out in the grounds, enjoying the gala. Hopefully that poor little girl would be OK—at least the paramedics had assured them she would be.

He helped Sadie unlock her door and realised her legs were wobbling like a newborn foal's. She'd pulled a towel around her tightly down on the jetty, although Fergal had got a good look before that. In any other situation, seeing some guy's eyes roving her body like that, he would have launched himself at them.

Now, in her room she dropped the towel to the floor and sank onto the bed in exhaustion. Then she gasped, her eyes full of horror. 'Oh, God, sorry!' Grabbing the towel up again, she pulled it back around her and he had to laugh.

'I've seen it all before,' he told her quickly, hoping she hadn't noticed the effect she was having on him, sitting there half naked in her knickers and bra. Her cheeks were flushed, but at least she was getting some colour back.

Sadie stood and crossed to the mirror while he lingered in the doorway. 'No, you haven't,' she replied after a pause. 'Seen all of me before...have you?' She looked wary now, as if she was racking her brains for something she'd forgotten. 'Seeing me in a bikini doesn't count,' she followed. 'Bikinis aren't generally this see-through.'

He bit back another chuckle, picturing the polka dot bikini she'd tottered around in on Hampton Heath that time he'd joined her and Callum and a bunch of other friends for a picnic. London had been so hot that day. Not as hot as Sadie, though. Callum had been watching Owen the whole time that day, as if he was daring him to look at Sadie so he could accuse him of wanting to hit on her or something.

It wasn't the time to tease her now, and definitely not the time to mention the way her nipples were probably the cutest little things he'd ever seen, pushing out against the lace of her wet bra. He should probably get out of here, he thought. But something rooted him to the spot even as she crossed to the bathroom in the towel.

'Need me to help?' he heard himself say, and then he caught himself. 'I mean…in case you fall again or something. I can wait.'

'I'm fine.'

Sadie paused with one hand on the bathroom door and he found himself looking at her feet, then tracing her legs with his eyes from her painted toenails to the rim of the towel, inches above her pale knees.

'I can probably shower on my own,' she added slowly, over her shoulder.

'You probably can. But do you want to?'

The words were out before he could even register he'd said them out loud. He pulled his eyes away, but not before catching a look on her face that he didn't recognise. She wasn't laughing, but she didn't look offended by his silly quip either. Not so long ago she would have rolled her eyes and told him to stop joking around, but now…

Now he was incredibly turned on, and Sadie had probably noticed.

'What are you implying?' she asked him.

He sucked in a breath, imagining his lips tracing the flesh across her shoulder blades under a steaming gush of water, his hands on slippery tiles, then on her bottom, finally tasting her...

His feet wouldn't move. He started willing his erection to comply with his wishes and not the wishes that would get him in trouble. This was the moment he was supposed to say nothing and walk away.

Just walk away, Owen. Go back to your room, go and get showered alone, and stop being an idiot, thinking things like this about Sadie.

'Owen, are you OK?'

She was looking at him in concern now, maybe reading his silence as distress on his part over what had just happened with Ashanti... And why did she have to look so gorgeous right now?

'What you just did...that was...' Sadie abandoned the bathroom door and walked back towards him, clutching the towel around her. 'That was amazing. I'm really proud of you, you know? That child lived to see another day because of what you did.'

'You did it too,' he said, looking straight into her eyes as her words lit him up and set his heart racing all over again. Genuine praise from Sadie, he realised, was something he lived for. 'Although you couldn't wait to rip your dress off in front of Conall McCaskill.'

She bit her lip and smirked, and instinctively he closed the gap between them and kicked the door shut behind him. An almost indecipherable moan escaped her mouth as she placed a palm against his bare chest, over his heart.

Her breath was a whisper across his mouth, inches from his lips. 'You're right. It's all about Conall McCaskill,' she said.

They were silent for a moment that felt too long—as something should have been said or done. She seemed to be testing the drumming of his heartbeat in her presence, and he was clearly failing to prove that he saw this half naked woman, beautiful inside and out, as just his friend and colleague.

'Conall thinks you are a hero too,' she told him quietly, clearly choosing to ignore the way he'd just shut himself in her room, and they way his chest was throbbing under her touch. 'I bet you never thought you'd see the day.'

'To be honest, I'm not really thinking about that right now,' he managed.

Sadie didn't move her hand. His heart was a riot, giving him away as much as the bulge in his boxers. Swallowing, he let his mind play out a hundred ways this could go.

Her hand on his torso felt hot as fire, and he knew without a doubt that she was waiting for him to do something now. To kiss her. One kiss. Just to see. Just to see if whatever this was, was real. And definitely not a 'friendly' kiss on the forehead this time. She wanted more. When a woman got that look in her eyes in front of him he was usually ready to give them more.

Her lips hovered close as she studied his gaze, then his mouth, as if she was tracing a prospective pattern. One kiss and he'd have to have another. He knew it. And another, and another.

'This is…' He stopped and let loose the tortured growl that had been building in his throat.

Sadie stepped away instantly. 'You're right,' she said quickly, flustered, turning her back. 'You're right. It's the adrenaline. I don't know what I was…'

'Get in the shower,' he heard himself say, flinging the bedroom door back open. This was messing with his head. If he didn't leave now he really would ruin everything. She'd regret it too—she was just caught up in the moment, like he was. 'I'll see you downstairs,' he said.

They'd have to talk about this later—there was no way they could avoid it. But right now it was better for both of them if he left and cooled down.

It took everything in his body and soul to turn away from her and go back to his room alone.

Sadie kicked herself internally more than once as she showered the events of the day and the lake water off her body. If only she could shower away the embarrassment and humiliation… What had she been thinking, practically asking him to kiss her...? Well, with her eyes and actions, at least...

He'd been joking when he'd suggested showering with her. Of course it had been a joke—to lighten the tension, probably. That was so Owen. Maybe it had just been his awkward way of making light of the fact he'd seen her in wet, see-through underwear.

She'd been trying to forget all the awkwardness, but the more they opened up and talked, and worked closely like this, the harder it was to ignore her feelings for her friend.

You have to, she reprimanded herself in the mirror. *Even if Owen Penner is no longer a notch on the bedpost kind of person, he is still your* friend!

She pressed her head to the shower tiles and let out a groan. This was all too confusing.

Her throat turned to sandpaper as she remembered the look in his eyes, right before he'd left her room...

The whole time she was drying her hair, a voice in her head was screaming. *If he really doesn't like you like that, Sadie, why did he shut the door to your room like that? Why did he look so tortured? And why was his heart freaking out under your hand?*

They had a problem. That much was obvious right now. Clearly they were both re-evaluating a few things. But what if she did get the whole package from her best friend and then he realised his mistake and snatched it back? Better not to even go there. God, no... The pain, on top of everything she'd already been through, would finish her off.

She sighed to herself, putting the final touches to her make-up, puckering her lips...imagining Owen's on hers. If she kissed him once she'd want more—she was just that kind of person. So for many, many, *many* reasons she simply couldn't do it, she reminded herself. Ever.

With that decided, she psyched herself up to see him downstairs, reciting a couple of positive affirmations at her reflection in the mirror whilst simultaneously admiring her breasts in the low-cut aubergine-coloured wrap-around dress. It was sophisticated enough for no one to question her professionalism, yet sexy—no one could deny it. At least she had that.

Was she dressing for Owen to find her sexy now?

No, of course you're not—don't be ridiculous.

Outside on the lawn, Owen was the first person she laid eyes on. He was chatting to the CEO, Dr Calhoun, and some of the other staff.

Vivek took her aside and thanked her profusely. Ashanti had made a full recovery already. His wife was on her way back from the hospital, having left the girl to sleep. Sadie told him she was glad, and then made small talk for about an hour with the guests…grazing from the buffet, purposefully avoiding Owen.

He was probably doing the same thing—although every time their eyes met across the lawn goosebumps broke out on her arms. A certain kind of ache, and a longing such as she'd never experienced before was threatening to snatch away all her common sense.

Some time later, the saxophonist on the marquee's stage was doing a fine job of remastering a classic, and she was so absorbed, standing next to Portia, that she was startled when Owen tapped her on the shoulder.

'Good party,' he said.

She crossed her arms. Her feet were already itching to move away. His cologne was too seductive—it made her mentally revisit the way he'd looked earlier, half naked in her bedroom.

'It's OK,' she replied, feeling Portia's eyes on them.

She walked towards the buffet table and busied her hands picking out an olive. Owen did the same, watching her every move, the picture of sophistication in his blue designer suit—an outfit she'd seen him wear on dates. A lot of dates. With different women, none of whom were around any more, she reminded herself.

'Are we good?' he asked, after a moment.

'I don't know what you mean,' she lied, popping the olive into her mouth and vaguely registering Vivek taking to the stage, and talking to the pianist.

'I think you do,' he said, causing a ball of nerves to lodge in her throat. 'Listen, Sadie, we need to talk about—'

He was cut off suddenly by the sound of the piano. They both spun around to face the stage. A beautiful piece of music she recognised was spilling from the instrument under Vivek's hands. His wife, now back from the hospital, was gaping at him from the sidelines in awe, wiping tears from her eyes. Conall McCaskill gave an enthusiastic whoop, and Sadie couldn't help the huge smile that broke out on her face.

'He's remembered how to play,' she whispered to Owen with pride, momentarily forgetting the tension between them.

'Come on!'

Owen grabbed her hand. Before she knew it they were on the dance floor, and Vivek's talents had extended into a slow but moving rendition of *Can't Help Falling in Love*.

They weren't the only ones dancing, so it shouldn't have felt strange at all, but the second Owen's hands landed on her hips the room fell away. She closed her eyes, testing her senses, praying for them all to switch from red alert back to their normal state around him. It was impossible. He pulled her closer, hip to hip, and as they swayed together every inch of her felt magnetised…especially when he lowered his lips to her ear.

'Did you want to kiss me up there in your bedroom before?' he asked her.

She drew a breath, pressed her cheek to his shoulder as her mind whirred. How the tables had turned! Hadn't she said the exact same thing to him after that night in the library? He'd brushed her off then, but the thought of doing the same to him now didn't sit right.

'I think I did, actually,' she admitted after a moment. 'But I know that was stupid. Thrill of the moment kind of thing…after what happened…'

'Whatever it was, I shouldn't have just walked away,' he replied.

'You did the right thing.'

'I bet you want to run right off this dance floor again,' he said, and she felt his smile stretch out like warm honey against the crown of her head.

'Again?' she replied, confused. But he'd caught her chin with one hand, gripped her hand with the other, and she forgot what she'd been going to say.

The way he was looking at her… He wanted her, she could tell. No question. Her blood fizzed like champagne in her veins.

'I don't know what this is, but we can't keep dancing around it, can we?' he said now.

Sadie swallowed. 'We should do exactly that—

just keep dancing around it,' she forced herself to say.

Not, *between it, over it*. Not *into it*. But every cell in her body was alive now, as if some new lifeforce had been summoned from the depths of her being, not to be switched off or drowned out. Talking about it was a bad idea. It would only lead to her admitting something she wasn't ready to admit—to him, or to herself. That she had a huge and ever-growing crush on her best friend.

This was bad. Very bad. It could never happen.

'You know what? I'm really tired,' she said, disentangling herself from his arms. Maybe if she excused herself, she could sleep this insanity off.

'No, you're not tired,' he countered, taking her hand again and holding it tightly. 'You just don't want to talk about it.'

'You're right—and I didn't think you wanted to, either,' she said, noting how goosebumps were travelling up her arm, the way his gaze bored into hers.

'We have to.'

Somewhere in the background rapturous applause for Vivek filled the air.

Owen lowered his voice again. 'We *have* to. Sadie, because we both know something's going on here, I can't even think straight around you any more. Something happened when I got back from Boston…'

'Nothing happened, Owen, and nothing *will* ever happen,' she snapped, begging her eyes not to give her raging desire away.

No one had ever looked at her as Owen was looking at her now. Enraged, confounded... consumed by the kind of longing she'd never known he was capable of expressing. Owen never wanted to talk about anything serious, and the fact that he did now, about *them*, fired her up and sent the fear of God rushing through her all at once.

'Fine. Go,' he said coldly, releasing her and turning his back to her.

Shocked, she almost relented. But why open Pandora's box now when it had always been just fine closed?

Quickly, while the crowd was distracted by Vivek taking a bow, she turned on her heel and left before she could make a huge mistake.

CHAPTER ELEVEN

OWEN PACED HIS BEDROOM, dragging both hands through his hair. Midnight had come and gone. He'd helped clear up after the gala—anything to keep Sadie's words from haunting his thoughts.

'Nothing happened, Owen, and nothing will ever happen.'

Weren't women supposed to be the ones who wanted to talk things though? Clear the air and all that? *Never go to bed feeling angry*—wasn't that what they said?

He ripped off his shirt and tossed it to the floor, flopping back on the bed in just his suit trousers, cursing at the ceiling. Admittedly his pride had taken a blow. Sadie Mills had abandoned him on a dance floor for a second time, and this time he'd walked right into it.

But they'd come so close to making out more times than he could count already. She was telling herself not to, just as he was, and he got it. Of course he got it.

There was no point in them hooking up. It

would only end in disaster, and more awkwardness than he cared to invite into this precious platonic thing they'd cultivated over the years. But he'd tried to do the right thing: get this blatant attraction between them out in the open so they could at least discuss it and move on, one way or another. He hadn't laughed it off or run away. He'd been trying to give her what he owed her. A chance to get their friendship back on track.

And all she'd done in response was close herself off completely. Was she trying to kill him slowly? It sucked, being the one given the brush-off, he realised with dismay. Maybe this was karma. That was what his mother would say, anyway.

Owen sat up straight. *Screw this.* He wouldn't sleep unless he saw her and cleared the air. This would only drag on into his dreams, into tomorrow. He'd just go and knock on her door, he decided, and demand they talk about it. She would not dismiss him.

Forgetting his shirt, or maybe just not caring enough to bother putting it back on, he felt a brute determination lead him to yank his door open. He was going to march straight to her room. To hell with the time—so what if she was sleeping? This had to end now.

No sooner had he stormed to her room and raised his hand to the door than the wooden panels disappeared in front of him and he almost fell through the doorway.

'What the…?'

'Owen!' Sadie gasped right in front of him. 'I was just coming to…'

'Talk?' he finished, failing to hide the way his eyes had fallen straight to her exposed cleavage in her nightdress.

She bit her lip, shifted on her feet. 'I told you… I don't want to talk about it.'

And before he could even gather his thoughts or protest, she launched herself at him like a rocket.

Her lips were on his now, her hands were in his hair, and she was kissing him as if her life depended on it. They staggered backwards against the banister in the hallway, fraught with passion. He hooked an arm around her waist, aware of the hard wood against his back, her leg around his middle, one hand on her backside.

Then a door creaked somewhere in the corridor. A voice came… 'Hello? Do you know what time it is?'

Who was that? he thought.

Who cares?

Owen pushed Sadie back into her room. Her mouth was red-hot, lips still parted, begging for more of his attention. She didn't want to talk, and neither did he now, as he let his tongue delve into her mouth deeply, then let it linger as they slowed their pace inside the closed room, but only for a moment. Then they crashed together against the dresser, making her hairbrush clatter to the floor.

Lips still locked together, he lifted her nightdress swiftly over her head, lifting her hair with it. The soft, sensual strands floated back down around their faces as his hands stroked her back and hips...new parts of Sadie he'd never thought he'd feel.

He wanted more. He could hardly wait.

Her bare breasts were bouncing in front of him now, teasing him as she started to unbutton his trousers. He shuffled out of them, bent to lock his mouth onto a pert pink nipple, standing up and ready for him. He circled his tongue around it and she arched into him, before staggering backwards again towards the bed, pulling him with her and muffling a cry of pleasure behind her hand before deciding it was pointless.

With a groan that was equally loud and equally telling of his intentions, he released her nipple, placed a hand behind her head, and arched over her on the bed, studying her face for the first time in this new situation. She was utterly breathtaking. A new version of his friend. Hot, messy, begging for him without saying a word.

He should back off. *So what if she started it?* came the voice in his head. But he couldn't stop now—not of his own volition.

He lowered his bulk onto one forearm and pressed a palm to the front of her knickers—the only thing left between their otherwise naked flesh. He was throbbing for her everywhere.

'Are you sure this what you want?' he asked.

'What do you think?' she gasped, reaching for him again.

As their tongues entwined around each other's he could barely think straight. Had she planned this? Or had she left her room to come and find him on a snap decision, like he had?

Who cares?

She moaned again, softer this time, as he slid his fingers down, circling her navel before going further into the fine, silken hair, stretching out the fabric of her knickers till she scrambled halfway out of them, leaving him to free her of the rest. She responded, exploring him with her hands, fingers, mouth, until they both knew they weren't going to stop.

'I know I have something, Owen…just wait…'

He ran his eyes over her in appreciation as she reached for her purse on the nightstand and scrambled around for a condom. She was everything he'd imagined, maybe even better. He urged her on to her back again when she had the foil packet clenched in her hand. He brushed his fingers lightly, tauntingly, over her mound and she gripped his shoulders hard, in a way he knew would leave circular half-moons in his flesh from her nails. Her eyes shone with new wickedness and a determination that sent an inferno through his blood as she locked on to his gaze.

Suddenly he wanted to possess her completely. He wanted to bind Sadie to him in every single way possible, regardless of the consequences. Maybe she was thinking the same thing. The way she rolled him over and took him in her mouth was nothing short of exquisite, as if she was trying to show him she was the best thing he'd never had.

'You are amazing, Sadie…'

'Shh…don't speak.'

Fine. There were no words anyway. God, he wanted her. If having her lips locked around his shaft was anything to go by, the act of sex itself was going to be something he would have to try very hard to make last for as long as possible.

That was not going to be easy.

Sadie's fingers pulsed hot and urgent against his hardness as they rolled on the condom together. He lifted his head, fighting the urge to ask again if this was what she really wanted. She wasn't backing off. Sadie was doing anything but that. He'd never seen her like this, so determined, so… *So not like Sadie.* He'd never imagined she could be so forceful, or that she could possibly want him. Would she regret this afterwards? Why were they doing this? It was wrong… It would not end well…

'Owen, make love to me.'

How could he refuse?

He positioned himself over her. Sadie was wet and ready for him, and she drew a sharp breath as he slid into her. He took it slowly, went inch by inch, in awe of every second as he went deeper... This was insane! His mind reeled, then went blank. All he felt was bliss, comfort, connection...

She wrapped her legs around him and held him still, clamping her teeth for a moment into his shoulder. Instinctively, he knew she wasn't asking him to stop. He stayed inside her a moment without moving, placing delicate butterfly kisses on her mouth, relishing the way she caressed his face with her fingers, stroked his hair. Their passion built again slowly, gradually, until Sadie was bucking under him, faster and faster, making sounds that made him want to spill into her with every thrust.

What followed was an exercise in mutual pleasure and gymnastics and still no words... They were just exploring and discovering and appreciating every inch of each other. The birds started tweeting outside the windows. The sun threatened to spoil the night and the way she moved in the shadows.

On the edge of her third or fourth climax, Sadie enveloped him with both her arms and her legs. He tried to pull out, to shift position—

why end this now? He wanted to prove he was the best she'd ever had too. He could make this last even longer…he had to. The sun was coming up. One-night stands had time limits. Sadie wasn't going to do this again and neither was he.

'Come for me,' she urged, her legs around his waist, gripping him even tighter, begging him not to withdraw.

This time he saw how tired she was, realised how sore she'd be once they released each other and…and what? Went about their friendship as if none of this had ever happened? What could possibly come after this for them? This was a one-night thing only. Wasn't that why they'd made it last all night?

With one final thrust he pressed his hot mouth to hers and heard a husky primal sound echo around the room. He realised it was coming from both of them, and they were coming together yet again.

The contractions made them judder and shudder and gasp, till he rolled from under her, breathless, floating back to reality as if he'd just been lifted up somewhere else and then thrown cruelly back down to earth. That had been like nothing he'd ever experienced—with anyone. That had been something raw and untamed and totally unprecedented. Mind-blowing. He almost didn't know what to think. He had too many thoughts.

He pressed his back to the sheets, finally allowing the softness of the mattress to lull him. His eyes closed. Exhaustion was an understatement. Sadie's fingers curled into his and he heard her emit a laugh of shock, or wonder, maybe both. He wanted to laugh too, suddenly. This was crazy. And reckless. Even now, when he was spent and sticky and tangled in her bedsheets, all he wanted was to hear her say she wanted to do it all over again.

Sadie's breathing slowed and he sensed her succumbing to sleep. As he let himself do the same, common sense crept in and started whispering at him.

What the hell did you just do that for?

Already the moment when he'd been free to touch her and cross any line he wanted was galloping from the present into the past, where it was morphing and twisting into something else. He could feel it already. Tomorrow there wouldn't be kisses and cuddling—not even if he wanted it more than anything. There would only be regret.

He turned away from her, so he wouldn't drape an arm around her sleeping frame and hold her tight for what was left of the night. He wasn't the kind of man Sadie needed in the long run and he never would be. She knew that. She'd just forgotten momentarily, that was all, and he'd gone along with it. If he carried on like this, disrespecting their friendship for the sake of sex, he'd lose her altogether!

Stupid.

Tomorrow he'd make sure they were cool—if that was even possible after he'd given in to her so fast… And he'd definitely make sure she knew that nothing like this would ever happen again.

CHAPTER TWELVE

SADIE SHUFFLED ON her feet in warrior pose, feeling too hot in the glaring sun that was streaming through the roof of the fernery. The yoga instructor had organised another hot session amongst the plants, and while she was glad of a little Zen, admittedly she was a little sore from last night. She could barely remember the last time she'd had so much sex in one night.

'And…let's move into our planks, everyone.'

Sadie followed the instructions, keeping an eye on her patients. She was pleased with Portia's progress. Despite her initial setback, the yoga was helping to strengthen the appropriate muscles around her head, neck, and shoulders. Relaxing facial exercises meant her episodic headaches were now fewer, with far more space between.

As for Vivek's hand-eye co-ordination—he seemed to be a different person after remembering his piano ballads the night of the gala.

The mood around the place was light. It was just Sadie's heart that felt heavy, as if it had suddenly taken on way too much. She kept getting flashbacks of the way she'd pounced on Owen in her bedroom doorway, the way he'd responded, and how it had escalated way beyond what she'd initially intended.

She also had a feeling Parminder knew. She was loitering outside now, on duty in case anything went wrong, but she kept giving her the eye. Parminder had heard them going into her room last night…she was sure of it. *Ugh*, she'd lost all control of her mind!

'And let's meet in our downward dog,' came the next instruction, leading to Vivek's disgruntled groan.

Sadie bit back a smile. 'You can do it,' she encouraged him.

OK, so he'd been happier *before* his therapeutic stretching session in the humid fernery, but soon he'd be Zen again. More Zen than her, anyway.

Her heart gave a little bunny hop as another flashback came for her—Owen's face hovering above hers, the light behind him outlining his strong muscled arms and chest, their perspiration adding to her wetness as they slid and sparked together.

A trickle of sweat dripped from her forehead to her mat. The memories were as persistent as a team of fruit flies around a glass of Pinot Noir. She could recall every single detail of the four times they'd taken each other in rapid succession, stopping only once for Owen to fetch more condoms as discreetly as he could from his own room.

Sadie shifted position on her yoga mat... closed her eyes. Each time her body took on a new shape she was thrown back to her naked gymnastics with Owen. She'd initiated it, yes but she hadn't exactly meant to. She'd been going to apologise for shutting him out. She knew he hated that, maybe as much as she did. She'd been on her way to talk about their obvious attraction, to get it out in the open, maybe even try and laugh about her crush in the hope that it would disappear, but she'd wound up doing none of that.

Just seeing him in her doorway, just as she'd flung open the door, shirtless, looking both furious and full of intent, she had felt something wild overcome her.

There was something to be said for not being the quiet, shy, serious one, for once. And maybe Portia had got her thinking about experimentation, but she'd been uncharacteristically spontaneous last night. The way Owen had always been. The way she herself had never been.

And it had felt amazing!

Even if she really should *not* have gone there with her best friend.

Portia had been right about a man never turning down sex...but she hadn't exactly given him much choice in the matter, pouncing on him like a jungle cat.

Ugh. Now what?

They'd already had an awkward 'good morning,' after waking up together. And maybe she'd made it more awkward by whispering, 'Thank you for last night' before he'd left her room. But she'd been nervous. They'd crossed some line last night and she didn't want to stick around to hear how he regretted it already. Or worse…that he'd enjoyed it and wanted to do it again.

That could never happen. This was Owen! Even once was one too many times.

'Sadie?'

Her heart pole-vaulted right up into her throat at his voice behind her. She sprang from her yoga mat as the instructor put a finger to her lips to shush him.

Owen grimaced. 'Sorry,' he whispered to the room, getting down on his haunches beside her.

Portia grinned at them from a cat cow position even as his familiar cologne made a knot of Sadie's stomach and sent her back to the way he'd tasted when she'd taken him in her mouth. God, he'd been so hard for her. Such a thrill…

Such a stupid, idiotic thrill to have acted on once, let alone multiple times!

'Ashanti's back from the hospital and has something she wants to give you before she goes,' he whispered. 'She's already said her goodbyes to Vivek, before this session—do you think you can duck out for five minutes?'

Sadie watched his mouth move but didn't hear a word he said. Every nerve-ending was alight again, just from seeing him. She wanted to reach for him suddenly, to reconnect, to feel some sense of reassurance that he hadn't forgotten what had happened, even though she herself had literally just decided to try and forget it and how different it had been from anything she'd experienced before.

'Sorry, what do you want?' she asked him when they were outside.

She gulped the cool air like a goldfish, hiding behind her hair, making a thing of rolling up her mat. Her hands were shaking.

He studied her, a crooked smile on his face. 'Ashanti? She wants to see you before she goes.'

'Oh, yes. Right.' Sadie met his eyes finally. For just a second she felt calm. Then the butterflies started up again.

'Are you OK?' he asked her, searching her face.

He was looking at her too intensely, so she looked at her nails instead. 'Why wouldn't I be?'

He urged her around to the side of the fernery, out of sight and earshot. Then he lowered his voice. 'Last night was… I wasn't exactly expecting that, Sadie…'

'It shouldn't have happened,' she blurted.

Owen straightened up. 'I know.'

What?

OK, she hadn't anticipated he'd agree so quickly. But they were best friends, for God's sake—it really *shouldn't* have happened.

'Sadie, I don't want to ruin what we have… or you.'

'Or me?' She frowned, letting his words sink in.

Was he insinuating he'd break her heart when he moved on—like he always did, at lightning speed? Was one night with her enough to restore his inner playboy?

'Don't worry, I know exactly what last night was about,' she told him, crossing her arms around herself, suddenly feeling smaller. 'We're both tired, and single, and far away from home. It won't go any further.'

'Maybe we just had to…you know…get it out of the way?' he followed up, cocking one eyebrow at her.

Sadie gave an insouciant shrug, but inside his words were scalding her and pouring ice-cold water on her at the same time. She was definitely the one to blame. Her annoyance was only with herself, over starting something that to all intents and purposes was probably the most idiotic thing she'd ever done.

Well done, Sadie.

'It was great sex, though,' he said now, searching her face.

'It was,' she agreed distractedly, swallowing back a sudden urge to blurt out what she'd been thinking all morning.

That it had felt like more than sex—to her anyway. That there had been a couple of moments last night when the pleasure of the physical act had been secondary to the closeness, to the soul connection. That had been something else she'd never felt before. As if she were so crazily intertwined with Owen on every single level.

It was probably all one-sided, though. *He* probably hadn't felt anything like what she had, making love to her. He was Owen, after all. Not only had he had way more sex than her, with more people, but he always kept his emotions out of everything. Why should sex with her be any different?

The gardener walked past and did a double-take. Sadie took a step backwards, realising she'd been standing less than inch from the tips of Owen's shoes.

'Well, now it's out of the way,' she joked, going in to punch his arm lightly for good measure. 'I guess we can go back to being friends?'

'I guess so,' he replied, but his eyes seemed to be making a data log of her innermost thoughts.

She straightened her shoulders, even as her

heart bucked and flapped behind her Lycra yoga top. It went haywire as Owen swept her hair gently behind her ear and examined what she knew was his stubble rash on her neck.

A look of dismay and regret crossed his face. 'I'm so sorry,' he growled.

'Don't be,' she told him quickly.

A little scrape or two from Owen's facial hair was not a promise. Right now it felt more like a scar. When would she be able to get *out* of here?

'I don't want things to get complicated…' he said, carefully.

'Mmm…' she replied to his lips, wondering why on earth she was still picturing him naked in her bed and feeling her core throb all over again. It was almost as if her body was completely unwilling to listen to her brain.

Very Important Friendship plus Sex equals Inevitable Disaster.

Catching her eye, he held her gaze and she found her heart thudding wildly as they played a game of who would look away first. What had they gone and done?

She followed him to Reception, where Ashanti was waiting with a bouquet of flowers for them. Sadie accepted the sweet gift and noticed every movement Owen made as he instructed the girl to always carry an epi-pen and told her that bees weren't exactly bad, just bad for *her.* He was good with children, she registered absently. She'd never really seen him with any before.

He kept catching her eye, sending more flash-backs to her frazzled brain. Last night had been so surreal… Had that really been them? Had *they* really done that? Had they really agreed all that hot, sweaty, passionate, frantic, soul-shifting sex was never going to happen again?

Of course it can't happen again. That was what you call a one-night stand, Sadie, and it was fun, but now it's done, so get over it.

Maeve wandered through to Reception with Conall just as Ashanti and Vivek's wife were leaving. She caught Sadie's arm and leaned in, dropped a kiss to her cheek, then reached for Owen's hand.

'Before I go, Sadie, Owen, I want you to know I feel like he's a different man because of you.' She nodded Conall's way and he simply shrugged and sniffed, as if it was no big deal. They all knew it was.

'We'll have some pre-exit evaluations this week,' Owen said. 'All going well, we should have him home with you by next weekend.'

Maeve lowered her voice, drawing them both closer. 'I'm planning a little something in honour of our son. We never had a tribute or a memo-rial service because Conall couldn't…well, you know. Anyway, I know it would mean a lot to

Conall if you were both there. If you could get away? We're in a wee hamlet not far from Loch Ness on the Great Glen Way. If you haven't seen much of Scotland I know Conall would be happy to show you. I dare say he'll be taking some more time off work...'

'Thank you,' Sadie said quickly, wondering how on earth she could refuse such an offer. Their home would be a mansion—the real celebrity deal! She couldn't help the excited look she threw Owen, but he frowned.

'We'll have to see what the schedule is like,' he said—to *her*.

'Of course.' Maeve smiled, squeezing both of their hands.

Sadie chewed on her cheeks, forcing a smile in return. Owen was being realistic. They were busy. A new patient was arriving in less than a week. But already she was panicking that he'd only said that as an excuse not to be around her, and now she'd have to go to the McCaskills' alone, without her best friend there to laugh at her over how starstruck she'd inevitably be the *entire* time.

That would be no fun, she realised. Owen made everything more fun. Including sex, now... apparently. Which was annoying. Sure, they'd acted like insatiable teenagers most of the night, but that didn't mean laughter hadn't sneaked in occasionally—like the first time she'd seen the hugeness of his shaft and he'd asked her, with a gleam in his eye, 'What did you expect?' She'd told him she'd never thought about it. He'd told her she was lying.

Soon it was just her and Owen standing in Reception.

'I should…um… I should get back to my class,' she said, thrusting the flowers at him. 'Put those in water, will you?'

'Yes, ma'am.'

She hurried back to the fernery, forcing herself not to look back in case he was staring at her bum in her leggings, or in case he wasn't. She didn't know any more which would offend her the most…

Yoga wasn't easy. There was definitely no Zen involved on her part, although her patients seemed totally blissed out. She couldn't get last night or her earlier conversation with Owen out of her head. They'd agreed it was a mistake, and that it wouldn't happen again, more or less, which should have been totally fine. It had been great sex. Undisputedly the best of her life—not that she'd tell him that. Why feed his ego?

Owen Penner was everything she'd always steered clear of. Unable to commit, allergic to love, renowned for distancing himself entirely from anything that no longer matched his needs or challenged his emotions. So wrong for her, in so many ways. Why think about it at all?

Forget about it. It was just a bit of sex between friends. It probably happens all the time. Stop making it into such a big deal!

By the time another night came around Sadie was practically chomping at the bit to go and knock on Owen's door again. She buried her head in her pillow, smelling his now far too familiar scent on her sheets, resisting the urge.

What if she suggested something crazy…like friends with benefits? That way she'd be in full control. She'd know it was just for fun, and she wouldn't be in danger of getting in too deep with someone entirely unsuitable.

Argh! Sadie yanked the covers over her head. What was she even thinking about this for? She wasn't going to be like the other girls he'd brought into his bed and then gone cold on. That wasn't in her plan—no, thanks. No more heartbreak for her. She'd gone through enough after Chris's death…

Owen wouldn't get close enough again to come even halfway towards 'ruining' her—not if she had any say in it. She'd be his friend, he'd be hers…he'd make her laugh, she'd make him laugh—that was what they did. She couldn't lose that. She loved it, needed it—she'd come to rely on it.

Getting their friendship back on track was all that mattered. Tomorrow she'd wash him off her sheets, she decided, and she'd wash that night right out of her brain too.

CHAPTER THIRTEEN

OWEN LOOKED UP as Sadie entered the room and apologised for running late. His instincts were on red alert the second he saw her face—even more so when she whispered that she'd just had to deal with a family emergency.

She took a seat and switched to professional Sadie mode in front of their new patient, a fifty-four-year-old lady from Dundee called Amanda Bond, who'd brought her Siamese cat with her as a therapy animal following a nasty fall down an airport escalator that had affected her in a multitude of unpleasant ways—not least giving her a fear of staircases.

Amanda excused herself to fetch the cat's food before the session, and he took Sadie aside.

'What's going on?' He frowned, realising his hand on her arm was the closest he'd been to her in over a week. Since their night of…whatever they were calling it.

She retracted her arm quickly and adjusted

her hair, as if his touch was acid, and told him, 'Nothing of concern.'

She was lying.

'So fill me in,' she said, picking up Amanda's file.

He bit hard on his cheeks, willing himself to stay on topic. So she didn't want to talk to him about it here—fair enough. But she barely spoke to her mum and dad, so whatever the 'emergency' was, it must be something pretty serious.

Maybe she wouldn't want to talk about it anywhere, he realised as she introduced herself officially to their new client—she was Sadie, after all. She was doing her best to go back to normal, like he was, but they both knew things were very far from it.

Every joke between them had fallen kind of flat lately, and as for the serious stuff—well, that had all been swept under the nearest Scottish carpet. Still, they both had a job to do.

'Her last neurologist put her through a four-hour test designed to make her face her weaknesses, then came to the conclusion she was faking the results because she scored too poorly in the memory part,' he told her.

'She said my scores were lower than a patient with dementia,' Amanda cut in, coming back into the room and placing a bowl of food down for the cat. 'I was just telling Dr Penner that I was prescribed Ritalin, anti-depressants and sleep meds. Not all at once, but… I knew none of that would heal me. I went to a cranial sacral therapist next, which helped with the brain fog, but I still wasn't *me*. I didn't know what needed when it came to therapy, apart from Sonny.'

Their patient crouched down to her cat and stroked its soft cream-coloured back. 'I just knew I needed something else. It was a year—a whole year—before someone suggested I come here.'

Sadie turned her gaze to him. Owen could feel it. He could literally sense her looking at him—a gift he'd honed since that night, when he'd tuned in to her and tasted parts of her he was starting to forget already. Which was probably a good thing, he reminded himself.

Focus.

'So here you are,' he said, standing up and crossing to the window, where the gardener was scrubbing something off the stones around the mermaid fountain. Rain was coming…hovering. Probably waiting till they set off later for the McCaskills'.

He turned to look at their patient. 'And you've been extremely patient this morning throughout yet another examination, Mrs Bond. We've concluded that most of your issues are coming from your eyes.'

'I suspected that all along. No one would believe me,' Amanda said incredulously.

He was about to reply but Sadie cut in.

'Dr Penner knows a lot about these things… it's almost like an instinct now, right?'

'Well, we still need to run more tests, of course,' he replied, turning back as his heart surged with pride.

Sadie nodded. 'Of course. But all those other doctors were likely ignoring your concerns about your eyes because they weren't specifically trained in what to look for when related to traumatic brain injuries and concussions. Not like Owen… Dr Penner is.'

She caught his eye and he wondered for the thousandth time why compliments from Sadie made him feel this way. They triggered something in him that made him feel accomplished on a level no one else could reach. It had been the same in the bedroom, he thought reluctantly. More than just proving what he could do with his tongue. It had become an almost instant need for her to want him, to be pleased with him as a whole, mind, body *and* tongue.

'Millions of brain injury survivors are basically disregarded by the medical community and written off as having mental health issues when it's all about the physical. We'll work together on a treatment plan,' Sadie explained. 'You're in the best hands here. For now, just settle in and enjoy some relaxation—it's all part of the process, right?'

Amanda beamed—the first time Owen had

seen her look genuinely excited to be here. 'I hear the yoga classes are great.'

'If you don't mind the heat,' said Sadie. 'Did Dr Penner explain how we'll be away for the next few days?'

'I did,' he replied. 'Dr Calhoun is scheduled to oversee everything.'

Sadie tapped a pen to her knee and caught his eyes again. She was probably as apprehensive about this time off as he was. They could hardly back out of taking up Maeve and Conall McCaskill on their offer to attend Scott's memorial, so rather than spending the time off for himself as he'd planned—hiking in the Highlands, clearing his head—he'd now have to spend it in a mansion with a famous film star and his social media star of a wife…and Sadie.

'I bet Sonny here will like this place while we help get you better,' Sadie was saying now, bending to stroke the cat.

He'd bet she'd love a cat, now her ex was out of the picture. Callum had had allergies—how lame. What kind of grown man was allergic to a little cat?

He caught himself. What was his problem, hating Sadie's ex even more than before?

Because you want her in every single way you had her that night, and you know you never will again, while he had her for years.

Talk about the longest week ever. He'd been

going to bed at night after satisfying himself in the shower first, just to numb the urge to bang down her door again. His back had burned from her scratch marks the whole of the next day, and the love bite she'd given him on his thigh had been bigger than the patch of stubble rash on her neck. Both had faded now. The last reminder that they'd done anything at all…gone.

God, she was already hard to get over. He'd made her come over and over and over and he'd been exhausted, but completely unable to stop. She was the first woman who'd ever been able to exhaust him to the core, and still he wanted more…

More than sex? It had crossed his mind briefly. She was different. She touched him…parts of him no one else had even got close to reaching.

But no. Why even go there? Relationships ended in misery for the most part, and their friendship was not going to end up like his parents' marriage. No way. It was far too good to watch it crumble into misery and hatred.

Maybe this time away as friends and colleagues would help them get things back to normal, he thought, with a glimmer of hope that lasted just five seconds before morphing into dread.

It would take more than a faded love bite to make him forget that night!

* * *

As predicted, it was raining. Owen watched the clouds swallow every other boat in their wake as the ferry bobbed towards Wemyss Bay. On the train across to Glasgow, where they were due to be met by the McCaskills' driver, Sadie was quiet, huddled into another colourful jumper, scrolling on her phone while the evening turned greyer, then blacker, outside the windows. They were alone in the carriage and eventually he couldn't stand the silence.

He tapped the glass front of her phone till she turned it face down on her lap. 'So?' he said.

'So, what?'

'The call with your family earlier on. Everything OK?'

She gave a long, exaggerated sigh and shrugged. 'My mother's in hospital.'

His heart jolted. 'Is that not…concerning you?'

'It's nothing too serious. She's having metatarsal foot surgery. It's just… I offered to go there, and she told me not to.' She held up her phone and showed him the text from her mother.

Owen felt his brow crease—it seemed the woman really was blaming her daughter for something to do with Chris's death. He'd been so sure—that Sadie had just been feeling guilty all this time because she had no one to reassure her otherwise. But here was proof, he supposed.

'Call her,' he said now, anger flaring up on her behalf.

He didn't know the full story, but if she'd offered to go to her mother and been asked to stay away...well, maybe there was more to it.

'I have. She said she has some things to discuss with someone first, and she'll call me back later. She's already decided she doesn't want me there.'

'Don't be ridiculous. It'll be something else— you'll see.'

He reached for her fingers impulsively and she let him hold her hand on her lap. A voice in his head said that he was being a comfort blanket... or a stand-in boyfriend till the next one came along. But to hell with it. That was what friends did.

He forced himself not to say anything that might sound like he was slamming her parents. He didn't know them, and they had their own set of problems after what had happened with her brother, but it sounded a lot as if they had no idea how the whole thing had affected Sadie all these years.

'You know,' he said, tracing a thumb over her knuckles, 'I really hope you don't think that just because we...' Damn, why couldn't he get his words out? 'I hope you know I'm not going to stop being there for you if you need me. I will never stop caring about you.'

A thousand questions flared in the grey of her irises when she looked at him. 'I know,' she replied after a second, before resting her head softly on his shoulder. 'That means a lot to me, Owen. I know you mean those things when you say them. You're a good friend.'

He toyed with how the word 'friend' felt now, coming from her lips. It was all they'd promised to be for each other, all he could offer her...only he'd never given anyone the kind of emotional support he now found himself offering Sadie. Weirdly, he was wanting to offer it more, even after sleeping with her, which was kind of new.

'Did you hear anything else about your dad's wedding?' she asked now, her head bumping on his shoulder with the train's motion.

'He wants me to go. I said I wouldn't,' he replied, prickling at the thought of it.

The invitation had come via email just a few days ago. He'd declined and had yet to respond to his father's follow-up email, asking him to reconsider. Of course his dad wanted his successful son in attendance, even if their relationship was far from perfect. The rest of their extended family weren't so bad—it would be nice to catch up with them, at least. If it wasn't for...well, *everything* else, he might consider it.

'Your mum doesn't want you to go, right?'

He frowned into the top of Sadie's head. How

did she know that? 'I don't do everything she asks me to—' he started, already on the defence.

'You love her,' she interrupted. 'You want to do right by her. That's who you are, Owen, and there's nothing wrong with that. But do you *want* to go?'

She lifted her head to study him and he avoided her eyes, shrugged towards the window. They were supposed to be talking about *her* parents, not his. Just being around his father made him feel like a treacherous son to his mother, yes, but also as if he should have called him out on his lecherous, cruel behaviour years ago, instead of bottling it up inside, letting the effects of it mark his own relationships, or lack thereof. He wasn't an idiot—he knew he probably looked at relationships through a warped lens, or at least a different one from Sadie, because of his parents. But he couldn't exactly unsee what he'd seen, or undo what he'd experienced.

'If you want to go, I'll go with you,' she offered now. 'Maybe if you take a friend with you it'll be easier...'

'No,' he said. 'Thanks, but no.'

Just the thought of it was like dunking his head in an icebox. His mum might not want to be there herself, but that didn't mean she wouldn't be calling everyone else for the gossip. He'd be forced to be a part of that tornado and its wreckage, and so would Sadie if she went with him.

Friend or not, she'd also get an earful about the Penner men's playboy ways, how his dad's weddings were now an annual event, how she should watch out in case she was next in line to need a divorce lawyer…blah-blah. All the usual jokes that weren't really jokes. It made him loathe the very notion of marriage and weddings in general… No, thank you. Hell, no.

'I heard your mum on the phone that day, out on the boat,' Sadie said now. 'She's in your ear all the time, Owen, dragging you into things. Doesn't that drive you crazy?'

He stared at her, then dropped her hand, embarrassment making him twitchy.

'Maybe you need to talk to both of them,' she continued. 'You're not a kid any more. They can't keep—'

'We were talking about you calling *your* mother,' he interjected.

Sadie bristled and tutted and took her hand back, slinking back in her seat. 'At least your family involves you, Owen, even if it is too much sometimes.'

He simmered next to her. How had this escalated so fast into another altercation? It was not what he'd intended, but she knew exactly how to rattle his cage—and he hers, apparently.

'Look, I'm sorry,' he offered. 'But I don't need to go to my dad's wedding, and neither do you.'

'Fine,' she huffed. 'I get it. You can be there

for me, but I'm not allowed to be there for you. No one gets close to Owen, huh?'

'I told you not to psychoanalyse me.'

She threw her hands in the air, then picked up her phone again, glowering into the screen. 'I wouldn't dream of it.'

Shame took hold of him instantly. He was hurting people with own stupid attempts at self-preservation. He was hurting Sadie now, by pushing her away again when he'd promised not to! She deserved more.

He ground his teeth at the window. 'No one gets as close as you've got,' he told her reflection suddenly. It was the truth. 'But you have your own issues, Sadie, you don't need to take on any of mine.'

His voice was so low and quiet it was practically a growl, but her head snapped up from her phone. 'I thought that was what friends were for—' she tried.

But this time he couldn't keep his mouth shut. 'Stop it, Sadie. This is verging on insanity now. We can't go back to being *friends*.'

'What do you mean?'

She looked dubious now, and even more hurt than before. He caught the back of her head and drew her closer, tangling his hand in the hair at the back of her neck.

'You know what I mean,' he said, even as her own hands found the lapels of his jacket.

He wanted to kiss her, to lower his mouth and take hers and show her what his tongue and everything else could do.

She groaned. 'I do know what you mean,' she said, almost regretfully. 'I can't stop thinking about it.'

'Well, that makes two of us.' He drew a deep breath, forced himself to release her. 'But you know I can't give you what you want, Sadie, don't you?'

She clenched his jacket, and unclenched it, and he almost expected her to untangle herself and agree with him. Surely she knew that. This was a warning. He was letting her off the hook right here and now. She knew what she had to do.

'What is it you think I want, exactly?' she asked instead.

'Someone who can give you more than I can.'

'That's such an *Owen* thing to say.'

'But I'm right. I know you, Sadie.'

They'd been inching closer with every word. Her knees were pressed to his now.

'Maybe you do…maybe you don't,' she said, her eyes glimmering with challenge. 'I'm learning some new things about myself lately.'

What?

'I don't want to ruin what we've got already but…maybe we should try being friends with benefits?' she whispered. Then she snorted a laugh and buried her face in his jacket. 'I can't believe I just said that to you. Is that crazy?'

'Yes,' he told her, even as he stiffened in arousal. That was the hottest, most unexpected thing that had ever come from her lips. He released her quickly, balling his fist. 'Don't you think we've made things weird enough already?'

'You're right,' she said with a quiet moan, long and lingering, deep in her throat. 'We probably shouldn't…'

The train rattled on, the rain slammed the windows, and for what felt like for ever he sat there, millimetres apart from her, in what felt like a battle with his own personal angel and demon.

Torture.

Do not go down this road, the angel in his head warned him.

Just do it. She knows it's just a bit of fun…she suggested it herself, said the devil.

He couldn't help it. Hot fire took over as his mouth found hers and in seconds she was straddling him on the seat, kissing him passionately in return, picking up right where they'd left off before.

Even if they hadn't been sitting in an empty train carriage, he didn't think they'd have stopped kissing. Except a train with all manner of filth and grime on its seats was no place to take things further. Besides, anyone could walk in on them.

Regretfully, he pulled back and she sighed in agreement, sliding off his lap.

On the platform at Glasgow he was still wrapping his head around what had just happened when Sadie clutched his hand and pulled him towards a guy with a sign bearing their names.

Halfway there she stopped and pressed her mouth to his, standing high on her tiptoes. He promptly dropped their luggage.

'Are you ready for this?' She grinned. A wicked gleam took over her eyes again.

Who was this woman?

Owen didn't know what 'this' was, exactly, but in that exact second he decided he was done with caring.

CHAPTER FOURTEEN

SADIE GAZED UP at the remains of the crumbled tower, imagining being out there in the middle of Loch Ness in the heavy winds that had taken down this castle's walls in 1715. Their tour of Urquhart Castle had gone ahead despite the rain, and she cuddled into Owen's arm under the umbrella, feeling bad that she wished the tour would be over, so they could get back to the warmth of a quaint pub and a hot chocolate.

She yawned.

Owen nudged her. 'Why are you so tired?'

'Very funny,' she whispered back.

He knew damn well why she was so tired. They'd kept each other busy till four a.m., and then the McCaskill housekeeper had knocked on the door at seven, urging them to get up for their tour.

Conall didn't have time to take them out again today—he was preparing for the memorial service to be held tonight at their home. But yesterday he'd driven them into the majestic Highlands, where the scenery changed dramatically at every turn, and where the pancake-flat terrain of the Lowlands was transformed into glistening lochs, forest-filled glens and craggy mountains.

Scotland was home to some of the most alluring scenery she'd ever seen. She'd almost forgotten it had once been a battleground for some fiercely territorial Highland clans... All she knew was that she and Owen were now embroiled in something so utterly fabulous that put all that gorgeous scenery to shame.

Sure, it was all spectacular, but she could just have easily admired the contours of his abs all day in bed instead of these mountains. She wanted it all before they were forced to get back to the real world, where they'd inevitably have to stop, and where he'd move on at some point, like he always did. Had he really changed? She still couldn't be sure... But last night. *Oh, God.*

She swallowed back the lump in her throat that warned her how tough he would be to get over. She'd just have to deal with it. She *would* deal with it—this was the new her! The new Sadie, who could be just as emotionally detached as him, and love every second of it.

Every time she'd felt Owen's eyes on her yesterday she'd had to resist the urge to touch him. They hadn't let on to the McCaskills that anything was out of the ordinary, although maybe word would get back to them from the housekeeper that her bed hadn't been slept in, she mused, once more zoning out of the tour.

She smiled to herself, tightening her arm on his, as the tour guide pointed to another crumbling wall and explained something about the nobles who'd partied there when it had been the Great Hall.

Talking of great… *What. A. Night.* Last night had possibly been better than the last one they'd spent together. Behind the closed doors of Owen's room in the McCaskill mansion she'd lost count of how many times they'd had sex. Once in the marble-clad shower, twice on the shag pile rug by the fire, twice this morning in the bed…

In that moment when she'd suggested a 'friends with benefits' arrangement she'd been trying to channel Portia, like before. It had felt so freeing, letting herself give in to her desires, knowing she was in full control.

There was also the small issue of her trying to forget the fact that her mother didn't want her in attendance at the hospital and wanted to discuss it with someone else. Whoever that someone else was… Was her mother in a relationship now?

She felt shame flood through her. Was she maybe using Owen a little bit? As a distraction?

The rain blew in on her cheeks and she turned to Owen, who moved the umbrella further to her side to protect her. Maybe she'd thrown herself at him on the train to stop the usual doubts and guilt over her brother from creeping in again. Every time she felt ignored or unwanted she did have a tendency to turn to the closest person for attention. She was probably doing it now, she thought, sniffing into the drizzle.

How many messages had she left her mum and dad so far? Three for her mum, offering to go and visit, and even one for her dad this morning. She'd had nothing in response except a short text message from her mother, saying she'd call later.

It was tearing her up, the way they never reached out to her. She and Chris had been so close. With only a year separating them, she'd sometimes felt they were more like twins. How could she not have known he was thinking about ending his life? He'd always confided in her about everything. Her parents obviously still wondered about that, too. She'd found the suicide note straight away, after all. It had been as if she'd known exactly where to look... It was all too horrid to think about, let alone talk about.

'What's that?'

Owen interrupted her thoughts by pointing at something in the lake.

'Is that the monster?'

She followed his finger, squinting through the rain, just as he nudged her again and laughed. 'My bad—it's another tour boat,' he said. 'You don't honestly think there's a monster down there, do you?'

Sadie shrugged. 'Anything could be down there,' she replied, just as a huge gust of wind snatched the umbrella from Owen's hand and sent it bouncing down the path towards a rocky cliff-edge.

'No! That's Maeve McCaskill's brolly,' she heard herself cry in horror.

Maeve had given it to her this morning—ahead of the forecast for rain. Before she quite knew what she was doing, Sadie was running headfirst after it into the rain, the abandoned tour group far behind her.

'Come back, that's Maeve's umbrella!'

The silly thing bounced and tumbled, a bright red blur against the stony grey castle. It seemed to enjoy leaping from her grasp the second it was within her reach. To her utter horror, it toppled towards a savage clifftop in a dramatic display of somersaults, and just as she took one more step forward, an image of Chris hurtled into her mind from nowhere.

Stop!

'Sadie, what are you doing? Leave it! It's just an umbrella!'

Owen was pulling her backwards against the wind, into him. She felt the breath leave her body in hot, short gasps as he urged her back onto the path with him, still holding her as she spun her head in all directions.

'He was just here, Owen,' she heard herself say through her tears. 'Clear as day.'

'Who?'

'Chris! I heard his voice.'

'No, you didn't—that was me.'

'I heard him!'

Owen's eyes had turned to narrow slits. He was drenched now—they both were. She sniffed in embarrassment, realising several of the other tourists were watching them. Quickly he led her away from all the eyes, hurrying her down the path past the group towards their tour boat, where it was dry. As posters of Loch Ness and the monster closed in on her he sat her down by a heater.

She barely noticed the other people staring as they started boarding and shuffling past. All she could see was Chris. Her brother. That was the clearest image she'd had of him in years. She could have sworn her late brother had just stopped her plunging off a cliff face—the way he had on his motorbike.

'I feel sick,' she told Owen, who bundled her closer and rocked her.

He said nothing as the engine started and they chugged away from the castle.

'You think I'm insane, but I heard him. I heard my brother,' she insisted, halfway back.

Owen still hadn't spoken. He'd just let her cry. Now he sighed hotly into the top of her head.

'You've just been thinking about him, Sadie, because of all this stuff with your parents…your mum going to hospital…and the memorial service later. It's making you think about him more. You need to talk to them—tell them about all this guilt you carry around with you. I bet they don't even know.'

She buried her head into his shoulder. Maybe he was right.

'Don't ever scare me like that again,' he ordered.

'I'm sorry.'

'You were willing to risk dying over Maeve McCaskill's umbrella? I mean, I know you're a fan, but…'

'Owen.' She turned to him and couldn't help but release a fresh batch of tears as they stung her eyes. 'I was starting to forget him. I was starting to forget what he looked and sounded like till just now. I miss him. I miss him so much.'

'I know you do.'

Owen looked awkward now, as if he didn't know what to do with her, but he held her as she sobbed into him on the boat.

By the time they were in the car, on their way back to the McCaskills' she felt utterly traumatised…but mostly by her own outburst. She hadn't been able to hold it in in front of Owen, whereas usually she'd have kept all that entirely bottled up with a lid on, where it belonged.

Back in her room, she undressed and stepped into the steaming hot shower. She waited for Owen to get in with her. He didn't. In fact, when she exited the bathroom in a towel he'd gone. Back to his own room, probably, to get ready for the service.

She kicked herself.

This friends with benefits thing was meant to be fun, and here she was letting herself get all emotional over her parents and Chris in front of him—what an idiot. He didn't need her laying all that on him. He had his own family dramas going on, what with his dad's wedding—which of course he'd be attending if it wasn't for his mother, always in his ear about what a screw-up the man was.

No wonder Owen kept his emotions at bay, after them *both* telling him that crying was a terrible thing. No wonder he felt awkward and had physically left the room just now, after she'd let Niagara Falls out of her eyeballs.

Well, she'd save him from any more of that.

He was happy to be fun summer fling material while she was enjoying being single and spontaneous for the first time in…*ever.* He wasn't here to console a crying wreck, and she wasn't about to let him think she was after another comfort blanket. From now on there would be no more tears, only fun!

Going for the black satin jumpsuit on its

hanger—something she'd been saving without really knowing what she'd wear it for—she wondered absently whether Owen would be wearing a kilt tonight, like all the other men at the service. Did men really wear nothing underneath their kilts?

Yes, focus on that Sadie. That's right. Just one more distraction is perfect—far better than actually facing your problems.

Her reflection seemed to mock her even as she dried her hair poker-straight and applied scarlet lipstick. OK, fine. Maybe hearing Chris's voice earlier, imaginary or not, was yet another sign that she had to initiate a certain kind of talk with her parents when they next opened the door for her to do so, as Owen kept saying she should. Chris would want that.

She should bring the guilt and shame that she and maybe even they still felt out into the open so they could say their pieces and all move on. What would she tell a patient if they told her the biggest block to moving on from something was their own fear?

The Mills family really had to talk this time, she decided, hands on hips in front of the mirror. Not like they usually did, about their cats, and what they were cooking for their respective Sunday dinners, and how the wisteria was blooming early. They had to talk about Chris.

CHAPTER FIFTEEN

MAEVE MCCASKILL LOOKED as solemn as Sadie had ever seen her tonight—which was only to be expected. The ten-foot glass dining table was laid out with her caterer's finest—for once, Maeve hadn't cooked anything herself. Sadie had offered to help in any way she could, and was dutifully helping to distribute little booklets with Scott McCaskill's face and birthdate on them.

She was standing in the doorway on the top step to the house, surrounded by perfectly pruned conifers, welcoming the drove of guests, when Owen came to her side in a green and blue tartan kilt, complete with plaid and knee-high black socks.

She had to do a double take. He quite possibly looked hotter than she had ever seen him look.

'You're giving me serious *Outlander* vibes. You'd better get lost before I ravish you,' she whispered, and he chuckled into his blazer and scarf, taking a pile of booklets from her. 'Have you got a musket under there?' she added cheekily.

'No, I'm just pleased to see you. How are you feeling now?'

'Better,' she said, blinking and shifting uneasily. 'Sorry about before.'

She assumed she'd probably scared him off… made an idiot of herself.

Owen sniffed. 'Don't apologise to me,' he said, turning her throat as dry as paper.

He couldn't meet her eyes now. So he *did* find it uncomfortable, her turning to him with her tears.

'Did you talk to your mum yet?' he asked, his eyes on the driveway, where a girl in leathers had just rolled up on a red Vespa.

She was about to answer, but Conall McCaskill was approaching in a matching kilt. He thanked them both again for being there, and for handing out the booklets. Taking one in his big hands, he sighed at the photo of Scott, running a hand over his tuft of a grey beard.

'Aye, he'd have hated all this,' he said gruffly, handing it back and gesturing around at the guests, some mingling on the driveway, some behind them in the house, others out near the stables—the McCaskills had seven horses. She recognised quite a few of them. There were actors and directors…friends of Maeve's who'd guest-starred on her TV programme. In any other situation she would have been more than star struck, but the excitement was dimmed somewhat by the occasion.

'Did you have a good day today, at the Loch?' asked Conall, his eyes glinting between them. 'Quite a romantic place, that castle, wouldn't you say, lad?'

That famous knowing half-smile was directed at Owen and it threw her off-guard. She compressed her lips, forcing a polite nod.

'We had an interesting time,' Owen said carefully, as someone in the rose garden, where the ceremony was due to take place, fired up the bagpipes.

Conall excused himself, leaving Sadie cringing.

'Don't worry about it,' Owen told her over the sound of the pipes, probably reading her thoughts. 'If they know, they don't care.'

Sadie couldn't read him. Did he care if anyone knew? Maybe not. Since when did Owen Penner care who knew about his conquests? That was what she was, she supposed. And she'd walked right into it.

'Nice heels,' he said, and smirked, oblivious, his fingers teasing at the gold zipper along the pocket on her hip. 'And that is one sexy one-piece you're wearing.'

'Don't think I wore it for you,' she quipped, seizing back control of her flapping heart, which was starting to feel like a lost bird in her chest.

She wasn't about to start caring that she was just a conquest now—she'd started the whole thing! But this was quite confusing. How *was* she supposed to feel around him now?

Don't be stupid, it's just sex. Feel what he feels about it—nothing, she reminded herself, before her thoughts could take her down a dangerous path.

The ceremony was beautiful. Sadie held her candle close as some of the guests made their speeches in the rose garden. Balloons were launched, candles were floated out on the lily pond, all overlooked by three marble statues of muscled Scotsmen on horseback. She learned a thousand things about Scott, a man of many talents, while she kept her eyes on Conall and Maeve, bowing their heads at the front.

She couldn't help her heart bursting with empathy for Maeve, for how poised she looked when she was probably breaking inside. Her mother hadn't been so strong at Chris's funeral…

It felt like so long ago, but also as if it was yesterday…walking into his room and finding that note. She'd racked her brains for all the things he might have said, the hints at his state of mind she might have missed. How hadn't she even noticed he was suffering?

But then, if it *was* her brother who'd stopped her on that cliff today, and not some perfectly timed memory of him, like Owen said, maybe he'd forgiven her.

If only her parents could, too, she thought, glancing at her phone for a message from her mother, as if one might suddenly appear, like Chris had.

Later, she was talking with one of Scott's friends when she got the call she'd almost been expecting not to come. As nerves consumed her she saw Owen watching her leave the crowd and walk towards the stables. It was quiet there. It smelled like sweet hay and expensive hobbies.

'Hey, Mum, how are you feeling?'

Her mother sounded strangely cheery as she talked about the friendly, encouraging doctors she'd seen after the operation on her foot, and asked about Scotland.

Sadie told her nothing about the developments with Owen—they didn't talk about things like that—but she told her about the film and TV award in the McCaskills' pool room as she psyched herself up to segue into the subject of Chris, wondering how best to do it.

Should she mention she thought he might have saved her today? Or would that sound crazy coming from a medical professional?

She walked through the sweeping stable doors, murmuring at her mother's words, and ran her hands over a smooth leather saddle on a mount on the wooden slat wall. Then, just as she was about to come out and ask why on earth she hadn't wanted Sadie at the hospital with her for her operation, and whether it was because she blamed her in some way for what had happened to Chris, her mother took a deep breath.

Then she blurted something so unexpected Sadie landed flat against the stable wall in shock.

Owen found her several minutes later. He cut a handsome sixteenth-century figure in the stable doorway, where he was devoid of any telling modern landmarks or objects.

'I guessed you were finally talking to your mother,' he said, striding purposefully to where she sat on a wooden bench, tapping her heeled foot against a box of riding crops.

He sat beside her, sending a shock of cologne to her nostrils when she didn't answer. She almost didn't have the words.

'What happened, Sadie?'

'He wants to be there for her,' she said, refocusing on the news she'd just been blasted with out of nowhere.

Owen looked confused.

'My dad… I think he freaked out, hearing how Mum wouldn't be able to walk too well for a while. They've barely spoken in years. She said she didn't quite know how to tell me…she had to talk to him first…but they got to thinking about it and they've decided to give things another shot. He's at the hospital with her.'

She must have looked as perplexed as she felt. Owen folded his arms over his chest, nudged an elbow against hers.

'Well, that's good, isn't it?' he said. 'Maybe he's just realised he needs to start looking out for her again. Do you think they ever really fell out of love, after your brother...?'

'I don't know,' she said, staring at a stray bit of straw at her feet. 'It felt like it to me. But I just don't want him to get all involved with her again, and get into her head, and then decide it's not what he wants. She's been through enough. They both have.'

She looked at him sideways then, realising how maybe it wasn't just her parents' situation she was talking about now. Owen's jaw shifted this way and that, then he stood and pulled her with him, till her arms locked around his broad shoulders.

She toyed with the fabric of his plaid for a second, and then he said, 'Did you tell her how guilty you've felt all this time about what happened? Did you give her a chance to tell you that none of what happened to your brother was your fault?'

Sadie flinched in his arms. She'd meant to start that conversation, of course, but the news about her parents' reunion had kind of cancelled it out. It was obvious they didn't want her around, though, wasn't it? Neither had asked her to visit.

'I will talk to them both together—next time,' she said resolutely.

Maybe she had taken yet another coward's way out of confronting them and her guilt.

You'd rather hide in Owen.

Owen's dark eyes were laced with doubt. She still wanted to hide in him, but that wasn't going to solve anything.

'It's not like you're my boyfriend,' she snapped. 'You don't have to take on all my drama. I wish I'd never told you I heard Chris before either… we're supposed to be having fun.'

His eyes narrowed further and his nostrils flared. 'You're right.'

'I know I'm right!' she said, even as the little white lie came back to taunt her. She'd wanted to tell him about Chris—needed to, in that moment.

She tried to step back from his unnerving, disapproving stare, but he clasped her by the back of her neck, tangling his hand in her hair.

'Then let's have fun,' he said, against her lips.

Sadie gasped, letting him urge her back into an empty stall. He kicked the door shut behind them with one shiny shoe and kissed her with such ferocity and intensity her lips and chin burned with the most delicious heat. She was flat against the wall now, clutching the plaid across his shoulder, her tongue dancing with his, her heels buried in hay.

Somewhere beyond their stall a horse snorted softly. The smell of horses and him mingled in her nose till she was so turned on by the thrill of what they were doing, and where, she could hardly stand it. She had to have him.

Her hands lowered to his kilt. Owen moaned against her mouth as she found his hardness under the folds, throbbing for her. So he hadn't worn anything under it… God, this was the most erotic moment of her life.

She shimmied out of her jumpsuit, noting the way his eyes roved hungrily over her body as she stood naked in front of him. Stepping forward, she was about to help him off with his plaid and claw his shirt undone when something huge and hard that wasn't Owen sprang up between them and thwacked her on the head.

'Sadie!' Owen made a grab for her as she folded like a card to the floor and crumpled onto the hay.

What the…?

Pressing her hands to her forehead, she checked herself. No blood. Thank God.

Owen snatched up the pitchfork that must have been hiding in the hay and tossed it like a poisoned rod to the other side of the stall. She'd just got bopped by a pitchfork.

'Lucky it wasn't the spiky end that got me,'

she said, as embarrassment turned her cheeks as hot as flames.

Owen was beside her in the hay now, checking her head all over, his eyes wide and wild. 'Are you hurt?'

'No, just mortified.'

'Would you just stop trying to kill yourself today?' he said in exasperation, before grimacing at his choice of words. 'Sorry, that came out… that's not what I meant.' He lowered himself to his side, checking her face again.

'I'm OK,' she told him, rolling onto her back, catching her breath.

Draping a hand over her forehead, she wanted to laugh, for some reason, but Owen leaned over her on one strong forearm, his eyes searching hers in concern.

'Owen, I'm OK.'

The seriousness of his face made her reach for him. She needed him closer, almost as if she had to console him for getting hurt in front of him— twice! Her fingers found the buttons on his shirt, and soon the kilt was cast aside and they were lying flesh against flesh in the prickly hay. This time he was less ferocious, more tender. She gave soft, encouraging moans as his kisses left a tantalising trail along her collarbone and his fingers traced circles around her nipples, moving down to the softness of her inner thighs, exploring her in the faint beams of moonlight peeking in through the skylight.

Dust from the hay swirled up as they moved and gave him an almost heavenly glow. His intensity turned her skin to goosebumps. Usually she'd be embarrassed, laid out like some wanton object of desire, but she closed her eyes and revelled in the way he made her feel sexy…like a goddess!

She was so absorbed in his touch and how different his tongue felt sweeping hers that she almost missed him unwrapping the condom. He must have been keeping it in his sporran, in case the kilt had to come up—or off, as the case might be. She almost made another *Outlander* joke, but when her eyes flashed open Owen was positioning himself over her and the look in her eyes rendered her silent. They burned into hers, devouring her whole, until she felt as if she was drowning in their depths, completely lost.

There was only them. Only this moment.

Owen rocked deliciously inside her as the hay tickled and scratched her skin, and she found her hands cupping his face, stroking his hair. She never wanted to look away from his eyes. Sadie could have sworn that she was seeing right through to his heart. He was letting her see all the way to the core of the real Owen, and what she saw almost made her cry.

She ran her hands over his bare chest and abs,

memorising the coarse, rugged texture of the thick, dark hair around his navel, committing to memory the feeling of having him fully inside her, and what it meant.

She tightened her arms around him, burying her head in his neck, breathing him in. So this was the difference between lust and love…between screwing and creating something sacred. She had never made love to anyone like this—had he?

'Sadie, what are you doing to me?'

His voice was all desire, all awe and need, as he rolled her over on top of him, clasping her backside, begging her with his body and his hands to ride him. She obliged willingly, bringing him to the brink and then slowing down again as he moaned into her mouth and kissed her as she'd never been kissed before.

She couldn't possibly have ever felt closer to him…or anyone. He said her name over and over, and the sound of it coming from his lips while they were connected like this made her feel a thousand things at once—scared, confused, powerful, wanted, *home*.

It was like being on a completely different planet, just the two of them soaring through some heavenly space, and after he'd jolted and convulsed in deep satisfaction she felt a kind of bonding with him such as she'd never known, like two turning into one. He clasped her hand above her head, stayed inside her, working his fingers on her till she bit down hard on her own hand, trying to stop vocalising her orgasm—it was all she could do not to scream the stable down.

'My God, Owen…' Her words came out muffled and full of her aching for him. She was coming so hard her knees were shaking, clenched to his sides like a vice.

Tumbling off him she fell to the hay, breathless, waves of pleasure still shuddering through her. Owen folded around her, his arms and legs like a cage claiming a tiny creature he never wanted to release. She smiled like a cat, curling into the warm hook of his arched pelvis, allowing this new flood of mutual pleasure and bliss to reach her heart.

And then he said, 'You really know how to show a man the benefits of your friendship, Sadie.'

She froze. Owen nuzzled into her neck. The party outside had gone quiet…maybe everyone had gone. How long had they been here? Why did he have to say that after they'd done *that*?

Oh, God. His words were like a blow to her abdomen. She felt as if he'd lifted her soul clean from her body, then slammed it straight into a brick wall. She couldn't help it…water pooled in her eyes even as she squeezed them shut.

Owen's breathing slowed as they lay there

glued together, and Sadie was glad her back was pressed to his chest. This way he couldn't see the tears that were clouding her vision, choking her throat.

That hadn't been just sex, or fun between friends—not for her anyway. It had been even more intense than the first time they'd done it. Maybe she'd wanted to hide in him initially, forget the world for a moment, but that had been making love—real, proper, soul-propelling, top-level, out-of-the-blue love stuff—and she couldn't even find the strength to deny it.

What was she doing? This was her all over, she thought helplessly. She couldn't just enjoy sex for what it was—her whole body, mind and soul had to turn it into something more. And now she'd gone and ruined things with Owen.

Blinking her eyes free of tears, she buried herself in his arms, memorising what it felt like to be there, knowing it had to be the last time she allowed herself to do it. She wasn't built the same way he was—what was the point pretending to herself? She was *already* doing what she'd sworn she wouldn't do—she was getting attached.

CHAPTER SIXTEEN

'Penny for your thoughts?'

Owen turned to Portia, who was looking the picture of health now—if a little windswept in her pink down jacket and jeans.

'I'm not really thinking much,' he said, casting his eyes back to the colony of seals lounging in the secluded bay.

They'd taken an afternoon trip to the west coast of the Isle of Bute, where Scalpsie Bay had drawn them in with its resident herd of grey seals, sunning themselves on the rocks just offshore. Sadie was further down, with Amanda Bond, who on this one occasion had been persuaded to leave her therapy cat Sonny at Rothesay.

'Beautiful view,' he commented, watching Sadie as she crouched on a rock, a foot away from a giant seal.

He was talking about her backside in her jeans, which he hadn't seen up close since the night of Scott's memorial in the stable, over a week ago now.

'How's your head today, Portia? I know you had one mild attack while we were away, but nothing since?'

'They're getting easier to handle, thanks to what you and Dr Mills have shown me,' she replied. Then she nudged him with her elbow, nodding towards Sadie. 'Speaking of Dr Mills…what is going on there? You haven't been the same since you got back from Conall and Maeve's.'

Man, this woman was astute. Or maybe he and Sadie were just too obvious. He raised his shoulders, stuck his hands in his pockets and motioned Portia to walk with him up the beach.

The clouds that streaked across the clear blue sky were turning golden at the edges in the afternoon light and the tide was out, for now. It was the best time to take what Dr Calhoun called a 'healing hike' in one of the island's top spots. The undulating green of the hills ahead was therapy in itself—not that it had worked on him. Not on this situation with Sadie.

'Things are complicated,' he heard himself say against his will.

It was funny, but he always felt compelled to open up to Portia on a personal level. Did Sadie feel the same, or was he just slipping up because their patient was a sexologist? She was definitely skilled at reading people.

'Complicated how? Usually it's people who insert complications where there really aren't any.'

He thought how best to respond. 'Well, we went from being friends to colleagues. Now we're...'

'Sleeping together. Is the sex good?'

Portia's grin took him by surprise. In fact, he was so struck by her bluntness he laughed. God, if she only knew the things Sadie could do with those full satin-soft lips...the way she could kiss. A surge of blood tore through his body and made him shuffle awkwardly in the sand.

'It's...well...'

'I knew it!' Portia clapped her hands in glee. 'So, how are you going to overcome these so-called "complications" together?'

'There is no "together".' Owen kicked up a stone, glancing towards Sadie again, who seemed deep in conversation with Amanda Bond. And then she caught his eye.

He had a flashback. Sadie lying down in the hay, her eyes searching his, taking him inside her slowly, intentionally. He could almost pinpoint the second it had stopped being a frivolous act of sexual gratification and turned into a level of lovemaking he'd never experienced. It had felt as if she'd let him in, admitted a trust in him that was not to be taken lightly.

The intensity of everything that had gone unsaid between them then had blown his mind—

even more than their first time, when he'd only felt a taste of it and then pretended it had all just been in his head. So he'd gone and cheapened it by saying something stupid, like he always did.

Either way, it didn't matter any more. She'd put a stop to it that same night. She'd practically run from the stable before he'd even got the kilt back on, citing the need to shower the dust off her. When he'd gone upstairs to her, the door had been locked. It had stayed locked until the next day, when she'd emerged with her bags and the driver had taken them back to the train station.

'She doesn't want to ruin our friendship,' he explained now, still holding Sadie's gaze. 'So there will be no more sex.'

'Rubbish,' Portia scoffed. 'She'll be back— mark my words, lad. You can't turn something like that off so easily once it's been turned on. So to speak! Besides, friends make the very best lovers. Trust me. I know.'

Owen dragged his eyes from Sadie's, wishing he hadn't been quite so open with a patient. It wasn't just unprofessional, it had dredged up that awkward conversation on the train back to Glasgow, when he'd asked why she was acting so weird. Sadie had told him she couldn't do 'this' any more. That 'this' was going to ruin their friendship after all, and she'd made a mistake. She valued having him in her life too much to make things complicated.

She'd done a complete one-eighty on what she'd initiated on the way there…as if one long weekend with him was all she'd needed for her 'wild woman sex fix' and that was that.

Was she turning into *him?*

If he wasn't so utterly confused he'd probably find it funny.

'She has a point though,' he admitted out loud, watching a speckled baby seal waddle out of the water and tip its head at them in interest. 'I would rather have her as a friend than not at all. She's a pretty special woman. And I'm not exactly her type, anyway.'

Portia smiled. 'You look exactly her type to me.'

Owen shook his head.

'Let me guess—she wants something serious, and you don't think you do?'

'I know I don't.' Owen inhaled the salty sea air as a flash flood struck his brain, sweeping up every argument he'd been subjected to between his parents over the years, all the family engagements they'd ruined with their petty war.

He hadn't told Sadie, but his mother had actually attended his dad's last wedding, at an idyllic winery near Bridport. She'd got drunk on rosé and taken Abigail—his father's last wife—behind a tractor, where she'd proceeded to remind her to hire a cleaner ASAP, because her new husband sure as heck wasn't going to do anything around the house. That had been just one item on her long list of things to expect or *not* to expect from a Penner man.

They'd been out there at least half an hour. Abigail had wound up in tears. His dad had had his mother escorted out of the winery.

'*They used to be so in love...you wouldn't have been able to stand that either,*' someone at the wedding had whispered to him, all while his parents were yelling obscenities at each other in the car park.

He'd stood there in the chaos thinking, *If this is what falling in love amounts to, forget about it.*

'I just can't give Sa… Dr Mills what she deserves,' he told Portia. 'She knows that. Anyway, let's talk about you, shall we? How's the journalling going?'

Portia smirked. She wanted to dig but he wasn't going to let her. Why tell one person about his inability to be in a relationship of any kind? It wasn't as if he was proud of it. But then again… his friendship with Sadie had always come first. Sadie had always been the one person he could count on, the one who wouldn't judge or mock or scorn him for anything. He'd gone to her for light relief from all the others…all the women who'd wanted more than he'd cared to offer.

Sadie had always been there for him.

Had he been a total idiot, denying himself a chance with her all this time? he mused to himself. Maybe he'd always wanted her underneath it all. Even before going to America.

But she'd only told him things because he was there—she'd pretty much said so. *'It's not like you're my boyfriend...you don't have to take on all my drama.'*

His phone rang. *Mum.* Speaking of drama…

Signalling to Portia to meet him further up the beach, he took the call, feeling Sadie's eyes on him again.

'Owen, your dad says you're not going to the wedding. I wanted to say thank you—you know your support means a lot to me. That man is unfathomably selfish sometimes…'

He bristled, stopping on the sand as she ranted about how hurt she was at not even getting an invitation—as if she could have expected one after last time! Usually he'd zone out, like he'd been doing for years… Only Sadie was still lasering him with her stare from afar, as if she knew he was letting his mother go on and on and on—like last time she'd overheard something like this conversation between them on the boat.

Fury made his blood run hotter even in the cool wind. Sadie was right. He could never totally zone out from this. This feud between his parents was the centre of his world, the reason for everything he'd put himself through over the years.

'Mum—enough,' he snapped, halting her mid-sentence. 'I love you, but this is toxic. Maybe I'll go to the wedding, maybe I won't, but that's *my* decision to make, not yours. I know you're still in love with him. Did you ever consider that's why you're really angry with him?'

Silence.

Then, to his utter shock, his mother started ranting even more. She was livid, practically possessed with her righteous rage. How dared he suggest that? How could he even think she'd still have feelings for someone so hostile and weak? Blah-blah-blah…

He sank to the sand on his haunches, tossed a pebble at the shoreline while she went on and on, and on some more. Why had he thought she'd take his opinions on board?

'That's your mother, isn't it? Give me the phone.'

Owen spun around. Sadie was behind him suddenly, towering over him, hand outstretched, hair flailing in the wind.

'Give me it,' she said again, just as his mother reiterated—loudly—how he was so selfish, just like his father.

He knew they could both hear it.

Amused, he stood and handed Sadie the phone, expecting her to hang up on his behalf. Instead, he watched in shock as she pressed it to her ear.

'Josephine? This is Sadie,' she announced, with an authority he rarely heard, but which turned him on instantly. 'Sadie. Yes, that's right. Owen's best friend. And do you know *why* he's my best friend? Because Owen is the least self-ish, most sensitive, most caring man I have ever met. And, with all due respect, he doesn't need you or anyone else to keep telling him otherwise. Now, if you'll excuse us, we have work to do.'

Now she was hanging up, as angrily as any-one could on a smartphone, prodding one finger heavily at the screen in an exaggerated swipe.

She handed it back to him, then crossed her arms. 'You're welcome,' she said as he slid it slowly into his pocket.

'You're my hero,' he said, and smirked, resist-ing the urge to tell her how aroused he was by her in this moment. She shot him a flicker of a smile, which somehow didn't feel exactly as if it came from her heart. 'I mean it,' he said, but she rolled her eyes.

He followed Sadie's lead, heading back to the slope they'd walked down to reach the bay, think-ing how he didn't know whether to be horrified or impressed by what had just happened. He'd bet no one had ever dared confront his mother like that before...no one except him, barely three minutes before Sadie!

Their driver was waiting at the top of the slope, but Sadie stopped just ahead of him, as Amanda let out a sorrowful groan. Their exit was blocked. Since their arrival a couple of workmen in yellow jackets had taken it upon themselves to repaint some lines on the slope. A glaring orange barrier at the bottom told them it was now a no-go zone. *Great.*

Owen strode ahead, waving at the guys. 'We need to get back up!'

'Take the stairs! Just walk around to the right,' came the reply.

'I can't take the stairs.'

Amanda was gripping Sadie's arm now, and Sadie was doing her best to console her. Amanda still had a deathly fear of staircases, thanks to her accident at the airport. Already her face had turned pale, the seals behind them on the rocks forgotten.

Owen tried again. 'Please, if we can just squeeze past you, mate?'

'No can do, lad. There's wet paint everywhere—sorry.' The man went back to his pot of white paint, but not before Owen caught sight of his name badge: *Peter Forry-Stewart.*

He did a double-take. His godmother was a Forry-Stewart. He vaguely remembered she had some connection to Glasgow, though the two women hadn't spoken in years, to his knowledge...not since he was little. Why, he didn't know.

'Your mother wouldn't be Aisling Forry-Stewart, by chance, would she?' he asked.

Peter looked up in surprise. 'Yes, that's her.'

Owen had to go—poor Amanda was less than happy behind him, and he could hear Sadie soothing her as best she could—but he took a business card from the man, for Aisling Forry-Stewart's Beauty & Botanics shop here on Rothesay, and told Peter he'd pay her a visit for old times' sake. Peter looked touched, but still wouldn't let them use the slope.

At the staircase, Amanda had gone from being slightly pale to apparition-white, and not even Portia's light good-natured banter and jokes would calm her. She sank down to the stony bottom step and at Sadie's instruction took long, deep gulps of sea air.

'I can't do it… I can't do it,' she mumbled.

Amanda was about to have a panic attack, which would be a setback no one had anticipated—least of all today. Owen had already had her on the tilt table this morning, where he'd utilised electric stimulation to calm her startle reflex, but now here she was, startled and shaken by the prospect of climbing some stairs.

She kept putting her palms over her eyes. Taking her hands gently, he crouched in front of her. 'You don't have to climb the stairs if you really don't want to,' he said, catching Sadie's wary glance.

'The tide's coming in pretty fast, though,' Sadie observed. 'There's only one way I can see of solving this situation, Dr Penner.'

She was right.

Owen pulled up his sleeves, not missing the way Portia and Sadie exchanged appreciative glances at his muscular arms in the sunlight. 'Do I have your permission to carry you, Mrs Bond?' he asked.

He felt Sadie watching him the whole way up the stairs, with Amanda Bond's arms looped gratefully around his neck and a crowd of on-lookers cheering.

Hero, Sadie mouthed at him, as he helped their patient into the car. He offered a mock salute over the roof, and for a moment it felt as if things were almost normal between them. Being her hero wasn't exactly why he'd done it, but if that was what she thought, he'd take it.

He was quiet on the journey back to Rothe-say, thinking how it hadn't exactly been a heroic move risking his friendship with Sadie for sex. He shouldn't have gone there. He might feel as if he wanted more than her friendship sometimes, but he had to remember what was more impor-tant. Her confronting his mother like that on his behalf—that had been crazy! It meant more than he could ever express. And she'd done it not be-cause he'd needed her to, but because she *cared* enough to do it.

There weren't many people in his life who cared that much about him—not when he flitted between lovers with barely a thought as to how it might affect them. If he ever did anything to stop Sadie caring about him he'd never forgive himself.

She'd given him a ticket out—freedom, singledom, the chance to move on unjudged, no questions asked. She'd given him what he always wanted after a few weeks of hot sex with someone new.

Yet here was the problem.

The thought of never making love to her again made his heart physically ache for her closeness, as well as a certain kind of fire start to rage in his belly... All the things he'd missed out on till now, going from one fling to the next, never investing, never allowing himself to get close enough to anyone to really *care* in case...in case he ever had to experience the kind of grief that came from losing someone he cared about, the kind of grief he'd watched consume his mother.

He'd picked up so many pieces over the years he was staggering under the weight of them all. His parents, with or without their acknowledgment of doing so, had rendered him so jaded about love that he'd openly rejected it, time after time, told himself he didn't want it for himself. He'd literally made himself believe he wasn't good enough to be anyone's boyfriend or husband. But he wasn't his father. He'd never let the love of his life turn sour and self-destruct.

He'd never wanted anyone as much as Sadie—

never even thought it was possible. Maybe he *should* ask her to his father's wedding, he mused. A date out in the real world, somewhere he could show her off proudly to his family—a chance for her *and* them to see that he'd changed. She'd know she was special to him if he asked her to the wedding. He'd never let anyone meet his family before.

CHAPTER SEVENTEEN

ON THE DOCK beside the lake Sadie sipped her coffee and swiped her tired eyes, trying to wake herself up. She'd barely slept. The banging in the walls was back, and this time it was louder than ever. Knocking on Owen's door had proved fruitless. He'd probably slept through it.

Thinking about it now, though, that was probably for the best. What good would have come from going to his room, to his bed, when she'd put a stop to that kind of thing ten whole days ago, on the train back from the McCaskills'?

Rejection was not something she handled well. There was no way she was about to admit she might be falling for him—not when he'd warned her he couldn't give her what she needed and she'd gone and ignored that warning anyway. They hadn't so much as touched each other since and she'd spent her nights alone, telling herself not to waste so much time thinking about something that was over. Finished. Done.

Her dad's name flashed up on her phone

screen, interrupting her thoughts, which were about Owen, as usual. Bringing her knees to her chest, she gathered her strength. He was probably calling to say how he and her mum didn't need her at the hospital, even after she'd offered— *again*.

Picking up the call and casting her eyes to the grey-skyed horizon across the water, she let him talk about the weather, and then asked after her mum and told him again how happy she was that they were giving things another go.

Her father seemed to stall.

'Yes, about that… Sorry I haven't called before. Your mother and I have been busy…and I know how busy you are, especially now you're in Scotland.'

Sadie's heart was pounding in her chest now, the way it always did when she sensed another excuse coming. This was why she'd been stalling on talking about Chris, avoiding calling them as much as she probably should. She couldn't stand to hear the fresh sadness in their voices over something she might've been able to prevent.

'I didn't want to bother you with coming to the hospital—you have enough of all that, what with your day job…'

'If you guys don't want me around you only have to say. It's nothing new,' she cut in, tossing a stone into the water—hard.

Ugh. She had to address this head-on—not

dance around it like she'd been doing. Again. Enough was enough, and she was way too tired to care anyway.

'I feel guilty enough, Dad, about what happened to Chris,' she said now. 'I don't need your fabrication...'

'What?'

Something in her father's voice made her swallow back her next words.

'Sadie, I was just going to suggest we all meet, the three of us, somewhere nice...when your mother's in recovery.'

'Oh.'

'We haven't really had any proper family time in a long while. We realise we've both made a few mistakes there. But I can't believe you're telling me you feel guilty about Chris. What happened was no one's fault—least of all yours!'

Sadie blinked at the lake. This wasn't at all what she'd been expecting and she cringed. Her father must think her a raving loon. She listened with an increasingly reddening face as her dad recounted with regret how consumed he'd been by his own grief for Chris, how her mother had shut him out and he her because of it—how they'd never intended her to get caught in the middle or blame herself.

The floodgates had been well and truly opened. They wanted her around...they wanted to talk about Chris together and remember all the things that had made him special. They hadn't meant her to feel this way for so long—just as Owen had said—they'd just thought *she* didn't want to talk about it.

Her dad even suggested she bring someone with her to their family reunion, if she wanted to. 'Maybe that nice man your mother says you're in Scotland with?'

Of course she told him no, that she'd come alone, because she and Owen were just friends.

By the time they hung up, all she wanted to do was go to her parents. This was a chance to make up for lost time, without the threat of self-inflicted guilt hovering above them all like a storm cloud. A thousand memories were ploughing through her mind now—all the times she'd possibly mistaken their wariness to interrupt her or bother her for a lack of caring. She'd seen everything through the perspective of her own guilt when she needn't have done anything of the sort.

Despite her total exhaustion, Sadie found a new spring in her step as she made her way to the morning's peaceful potting session. She was excited to tell Owen what had just happened. He'd roll his eyes, tell her he'd known all along she had nothing to worry about, she knew it. He'd do all the things a good friend would do.

She just needed to stop wanting to sleep with him more than she ever had before, she thought, grimacing at her shoes as she crossed the dewy lawn. Or wondering what it might be like for him to meet her parents. They'd love him. He always made things more interesting.

There was nothing like sexual abstinence to make the heart grow fonder, she thought with a sigh, tossing her coffee cup into the trash on her way into the fernery.

Parminder called Sadie over the second she stepped foot inside the heat-soaked Victorian glasshouse. 'Did you see this?' she asked excitedly, waving what looked like the local newspaper in the air above her head.

Intrigued, Sadie took the paper—then felt her eyes bulge.

Someone at the bay had witnessed their little escapade with the stairs the other day and had sent a photo in. Apparently Owen's actions had started a small quest amongst the locals to determine who the 'hero' was who'd carried the 'sick woman' up the stairs, and now Owen's bulging biceps were a prominent feature on page two.

'Oh, he's going to love this,' she said, smiling to herself at the photo.

Those arms around her had felt so right…like a barrier against the world.

Maybe it wouldn't be such a stupid idea—fessing up to her feelings. Anything that consumed her thoughts like this was worth fighting for, wasn't it?

She took a seat at the round table under the indoor palms. Was he missing her at night too and just didn't know how to say it? She had been the one to end things after all—and rather abruptly at that. What if she just owned up to the fact that she'd been too afraid to like him? *Really* like him. Maybe even love him. In case he ever changed his mind.

Either he felt the same, and they could try and make a go of things, or he didn't. In which case she'd do her very best to keep him as her closest friend. It would be hard. Probably impossible. But if she didn't at least talk to him, take a risk, she'd never know what might've been.

'Going to love what?'

Owen had walked in behind them with Vivek and Portia, ready for this, their last activity. Both were being discharged that afternoon. Sadie groaned internally at how handsome he looked today in his uniform as he pulled out a chair for Portia.

'You're famous,' Parminder said, beaming.

She took the paper from Sadie's hands and placed it on the table so they could all see it. Owen's face was unreadable, but Sadie knew he was secretly loving the acclaim.

'You're the hero of Rothesay now,' Parminder teased him as he took a seat.

The fernery was hot today. The sun was streaming through the roof and windows and

Sadie hoped she didn't look as tired as she felt as she fanned her face.

'Is that where you went last night?' Parminder asked Owen. 'Off with one of your new admirers? I saw you coming back late again... What was it? Two a.m.? I couldn't sleep, as usual.'

Sadie balked. *What?*

'I don't have any new admirers,' he answered coyly, swiping a pot from the centre of the table and handing a packet of seeds to Portia.

Something in his voice sent a red flag waving in Sadie's mind. He couldn't even look at her now. He was hiding something.

Oh, my God.

He hadn't been asleep when she'd knocked. He hadn't even been there!

A wave of nausea swept through her belly and lodged in her throat. There she'd been, just seconds ago, fantasising that maybe...just maybe... she could change him. That he might just want to try and be boyfriend material for her. *Idiot.*

Owen's eyes penetrated hers across the table the whole time they were potting plants, but she couldn't look at him. She'd told him she valued his friendship too much to risk ruining it, and that was true... But now she burned for the other parts of him.

The Owen who comforted her and protected her and gave her the best advice out of all her friends. The Owen who could make her laugh and minutes later make her tremble in awe and wonder at all his previously hidden talents. She physically ached for him, especially now she was picturing him with someone else. *Already.*

Suddenly the shock of Parminder's revelation twisted into fury. Sadie bit hard on her cheeks and tongue, then rammed a seed so hard into a plant pot her finger shot through the bottom of it. He was seeing someone else. *Already.*

Portia's brow was furrowed as she looked in her direction. 'Are you OK, Dr Mills?'

This was no good. Sadie pushed her chair back. 'I just remembered I have some paperwork to attend to. Dr Penner will finish up with you. Please excuse me.'

She couldn't be near him a moment longer. All she could see in her mind's jealous eye was him cosied up with some woman in the town—some admirer he'd turned to the second she'd put a stop to their 'benefits'.

Hurrying back to the house, she busied herself with discharge paperwork she could easily have done after the session, despite her shaky hands. This was always going to happen. He was always going to move on. She knew that. This was Owen! This was what he did.

Let him go, she told herself.

But her bottom lip and her chin insisted on wobbling, and her tears blurred the paperwork. Folding her head onto her arms on the desk, she sobbed as she hadn't sobbed since that day on the loch after she'd thought she'd heard Chris. Deep, soul-crushing, lung-busting, body-shaking sobs.

This was the moment she'd feared most—the reason she'd been off and on with this arrangement since the start. She was crying over Owen.

God, she'd been a total idiot, falling for the most notorious player she'd ever known, giving him all of herself, knowing deep down she was putting her stupid soft heart in the firing line. She'd fallen harder than she'd even thought, without ever meaning to, and he hadn't even been able to wait five minutes to hook up with someone else!

One cry, she told herself as she sniffed behind the closed study door. *One cry and then you're done. He will never know this happened. You will not waste your tears on him!*

Sadie hoped she was managing to appear unfazed when, a few hours later, Owen took her aside on the front steps.

'It's pretty sad to see them go, isn't it?' he said to her. The driver was here to take Portia and Vivek to the train station with their bags, and they were bidding them a warm farewell with promises of follow-up video calls over the next few weeks.

Just as she was about to descend the steps in her floral shirt and capris, a lipstick-wearing, radiant-looking Portia took Sadie aside. 'I want updates on *you*,' she said, pursing her lips, then glancing sideways at Owen. 'Don't think we're not all rooting for you.'

Even Vivek seemed to be holding back a smile as he looked her way from where he was shaking hands with Owen. Were they all talking about them? she wondered, deciding it was better not to think about it.

'You've helped us more than you know,' Portia said, her kind eyes twinkling. 'I hope you do something nice for yourself where that one is concerned.'

'Owen and I are most definitely just colleagues,' Sadie reminded her, and not for the first time. Although now the words bore a certain heaviness after all the what-ifs and maybes of the past few weeks.

They said their final goodbyes, which was indeed quite emotional for Sadie after all this time of getting to know her patients. She was going to miss Portia's little insights, as invasive as they sometimes were.

Sadie was all set to get back to work on Amanda's new schedule when Owen cornered her in the hallway.

'Sadie?'

His hand on her wrist made all the blood rush to her head and she froze, instantly picturing his hands on someone else.

Quickly, she pulled her hand back. 'I'm pretty busy, Owen…'

'I just wanted to tell you I've decided to go to Dad's wedding,' he said, dashing a hand through his hair.

'Good for you,' she responded, a little more coldly than she'd planned.

He didn't seem to notice.

'I was thinking maybe…' Owen trailed off, shaking his head.

He folded his arms across his chest and stepped aside for Fergal, who was pulling the luggage trolley back towards them from the doorway. Was it her imagination, or did Owen look sheepish? She straightened her back. Of course he probably felt bad for sleeping with someone else so soon, but that was his prerogative, she supposed. He could do what he liked.

'What's wrong?' he asked her now, and she realised she was scowling deeply at the space between his eyes, digging her nails into her palms, imagining him in his tux at the wedding, looking dreamy as hell…checking all the women out, no doubt.

'Nothing's wrong. I told you—I'm busy,' she said, feigning a smile she knew probably hadn't made it to her eyes. 'What were you thinking?'

He looked at her long and hard, as if something heavy was percolating in his brain. She braced herself to hear who he was taking to the wedding—because it sure as heck wasn't going to be her now he'd moved on.

'Forget about it,' he said eventually.

Great. As if she would.

If only her heart wasn't going a million miles an hour. Maybe he wasn't taking anyone at all. Why should she care? Especially now, when there was nothing between them but some vague and twisted form of friendship—what was left of it, that was. It had only ever been going to end this way, with her a mess and him absolutely fine.

'You're angry at me for something,' he accused her now. 'Out with it.'

'Don't be ridiculous,' she shot back.

He huffed a laugh. 'So we're right back here, are we?'

She pulled her eyes away from his challenging stare. That time he'd accused of her being jealous—of Parminder of all people—she'd laughed him off. He knew when she was jealous! He probably knew she was now. But if she voiced her concerns about whoever he was meeting at night, he'd ask her what right she had to question him when *she'd* called things off. Besides, he hadn't made any promises to her. He wasn't exactly in the habit of making promises to anyone—that was why she'd called it off!

Unless... He does look pretty angry. Did you just jump the gun? This is all such a mess!

Owen was still simmering at her. The hallway closed in even further. Even the fountain outside seemed to fall silent.

'You don't want to talk to me?' he asked.

Before she could get her head straight and form a sentence, he threw his hands in the air.

'You know what? If you still don't want to talk to me about anything real, Sadie, maybe we should think about ending *everything* between us—including this so-called friendship.'

His words left her cold. She was still grappling for speech when he brushed straight past her and stormed up the stairs.

CHAPTER EIGHTEEN

SADIE SQUINTED AT the map app on her phone and took a left, as instructed. For all the time she'd been at Rothesay Recovery, she hadn't exactly spent much time in the town itself, but she needed to post a card to her mother, and it only felt right to do it herself on this Saturday morning instead of handing it to someone at Rothesay.

She'd also seen Owen leave a few minutes before her…

The birds in the trees seemed to be judging her as she took the path towards the row of shops, along the harbour. 'Stop it, birds. It's not like I'm following him,' she said, and tutted at them.

Well, she wasn't. Not really. That would be silly.

OK, fine, she was kind of following him. To see where he'd gone… To see if she was right and he *was* with some new lady friend. Only she'd stopped to check the map and the next thing she knew he'd disappeared. And now she was just feeling silly—and guilty.

The hungry seagulls swirled overhead, squawking into her thoughts and only momentarily blocking the vision of Owen's face...how angry he'd looked yesterday. He'd accused her of not wanting to talk about anything real! But it was *too* real, knowing he'd moved on so fast. How was she supposed to talk about that?

No one had ever made her feel so heartsick, so angry, so entirely impassioned and...scared. She wanted him...wanted nothing more than to tell him how she felt, which was jealous as hell. But what if...?

What if...?

What if he *did* feel the same, and they got together, and then he changed his mind?

That was the real reason she'd said nothing when he'd challenged her. The real reason she'd tried so hard not to fall for him in the first place.

She sighed long and hard, staring at the mountains ahead. As usual, she'd cut off her own nose to spite her face and that was why she'd followed him. To find him and tell him once and for all how she felt. Madly, jealously, in love with him?

This was what Portia had been talking about, she thought, stopping to rest her arms against the high brick wall around the harbour. Three white boats bobbed in the gentle breeze, while behind them the tops of the rolling hills were swallowed by clouds. It seemed fitting for her clouded brain.

She'd found someone who fulfilled every part of her. None of the other men in her life had come close to making her feel like Owen did, which was exactly why she'd felt safe with them. None of them had ever had the capacity to break her the way losing Chris had broken her.

The way losing Owen would break her.

She snapped a photo of a speckled brown bird that had flown onto the wall beside her. A cute young couple had stopped a few feet away and were kissing over their coffee cups.

Callum was back in her head now...their last goodbye and how it had ended. There hadn't even been a row. She'd been stunned by his announcement, and reduced to tears by the sudden rejection—not a thing she'd ever handled well—but she hadn't been broken.

It hadn't been a powerful love with him, she supposed. Not the kind of love he deserved or *she* deserved. Definitely not the kind she'd tasted with Owen. This was something real... And maybe it was time to trust herself to deal with it and not be so scared by the thought of something else ending that she hadn't even let it begin!

The bird flew away and came to a new perching position on one of the boats. Frowning at the water, and hugging her jacket around herself more tightly, she wondered why on earth she'd let it go this far—pushing away the only person in the whole world she could stand to be around twenty-four-seven. Maybe even pushing him unwittingly towards someone else.

She pressed on, away from the harbour towards the post office, nodding to a passing dogwalker with a German Shepherd. There was still no sign of Owen, but as she rounded the corner something caught her eye. A small shop with a green-and-white-striped frontage: Beauty & Botanics. Something about the name was familiar, but what?

Oh, yes. Owen had a business card from there. She'd seen it sticking out of his back pocket, that day he'd carried Amanda up the stairs. She hadn't thought anything of it at the time, but… Oh, God. Was he with someone else right now?

Someone who worked in this shop?

Owen hadn't exactly meant to burden this woman with the details of his current situation when he'd taken it upon himself to pay her a visit, but he was grateful for someone unbiased to listen. It felt like a long time since he'd spoken to anyone outside of Rothesay Recovery, or anyone who didn't know Sadie, for that matter.

He stood up from one of the two plush green velvet seats by the shop window to accept the cup of mint tea Aisling handed him. This was his second visit. The first, of course, had been the other night, when he'd somehow got so caught in the catch-up and conversation with his god-mother that he'd lost all track of time.

'So, tell me, where did we leave off?' she said now, swiping her long grey-blonde hair over one shoulder and lighting a candle.

The smell of lemongrass mingled with the posh soaps and other products dotted amongst the plants. It was as Zen as the fernery in here—like a five-star version

Aisling was a wisp of a woman, the same slen-der build as his mother. The two had gone to school together and drifted apart after his mum's divorce.

'Did you ask your friend Sadie to your dad's wedding?' she asked.

Owen glowered for a moment into his teacup and forgot his Zen. 'I started to...' He paused, remembering the look on her face, filled with all the accusations she'd been storing up unspo-ken, her eyes burning into him like red-hot pok-ers. 'I think she thinks I've moved on from her, but she's too stubborn to ask because *she* ended things and she doesn't want to look jealous. I know her, Aisling. I know her better than she knows herself.'

Aisling nodded slowly, thoughtfully. 'If you know she's jealous, and it's eating you both up, the question is, Owen Penner, what are you going to do about it?'

Owen sat back down, stirred his teabag around by the string. It wasn't as if he hadn't been thinking about that ever since. All of it—everything they'd done over the last few weeks. The times when he'd dissolved into her, let her claim him fully. He'd never done that with anyone—never even dared to let someone that close.

Now he knew he was capable of it, he wanted to do it again and again. But she didn't trust him. Of course she didn't trust him. He hadn't fought for her when he'd had the chance. He'd backed off, as she'd asked. He shouldn't have done that—shouldn't for one second have let her think he was putting her in the same 'been there, done that' category as the other women she'd seen him get bored with.

He'd been trying to be respectful, to keep their friendship alive. But what a joke. He didn't want her at his dad's wedding as his friend—he wanted to show her off and kiss her and dance with her, knowing she wouldn't run from the dance floor this time…knowing she'd stay in his arms where she belonged.

'I want to be with Sadie,' he heard himself say now. 'She doesn't trust me not to hurt her, and I didn't trust myself not to either—not for a long time. But I know I'd never do that…not any more.' He put his cup down on the little dresser by the door. 'I couldn't. I love her, Aisling. I really do. And you have no idea how weird it is to hear myself say that out loud.'

He wrung his hands together on his knees. It felt as if a lead iron weight had been lifted from his shoulders, just knowing he could actually say something like that and mean it.

'She doesn't think I can give her what she needs, and I don't blame her after all this time, but it's different with her.'

Aisling was smiling. 'If she's the one, everything will feel different. You know, your mother tore herself apart over your father. I saw the way that love destroyed her. That was a different kind of love, Owen. It put me off the whole notion of being with someone for a long time…maybe that's why your mother and I drifted apart.'

She cocked an eyebrow, studying him intently as she stroked a finger over a row of fancy-looking lotion bottles. Owen was floored. His own mother had lost her friend because of her issues with his dad? It was just like Sadie said: he'd been preparing himself for the worst in relationships his whole life—never getting into one, telling himself he didn't want one! Choosing to believe love was a waste of time…

But deep down he'd probably always just been waiting for Sadie.

Owen almost laughed as the shock set in. There would never be a time he wouldn't want to laugh with Sadie, make love to her, fight with her! He could live in that cycle his whole life and never get bored.

'I was about to tell her once…how much I liked her,' he said now. 'I almost kissed her. We were twenty-two—can you believe that? She ran off the dance floor before I had the chance. I told myself I was glad, because I would've ruined a good friendship—you don't get drunk and kiss your friends! I hooked up with someone else to get her off my mind, and the next thing I knew I was stuck in the friend zone permanently.'

'You wanted to kiss me that night in the club?'

Sadie's voice behind him sent his stomach plunging to the floor. She'd appeared in the doorway like a ghost, in jeans and a cashmere sweater. Owen got to his feet, stunned. How long had she been there?

He cleared his throat, dashed a hand to his hair. How much had she heard?

'I did,' he admitted. 'Actually, since the moment I flicked ink at you…on purpose.'

'Owen!'

She put her hands over her face, but he took them in his in a second, and Aisling crept into the back of the shop, to give them privacy.

'I can't believe this,' Sadie whispered, swiping at her eyes.

He pulled her closer, scooping her face towards his, close enough to taste her lips again. But she was talking.

'I came to try and find you…to tell you I'm an idiot, that I miss my best friend and I don't want to lose him. But I miss the man who loves me the way you do *more*. I want both, Owen.'

Owen's heart was a riot as he scanned her eyes. 'I want to be both of those things for you,' he said, without looking away.

He knew now, with no trace of uncertainty that he'd do anything for her and go anywhere with her.

'Maybe I was too scared to admit I liked you back then,' Sadie said now, turning his hands in hers. 'Maybe I got stupidly drunk that night, trying to feel brave enough to kiss you first. But I was so drunk that I ran away and threw up. And then…'

She paused, biting on her lip, and he might have laughed, if it hadn't been for the giant lump blocking his throat.

'Owen, we would never be here now if we hadn't been best friends first.'

'Trust me… I know,' he managed, bringing her hand up to kiss her fingers.

Outside, someone reconsidered entering the

shop and he swept her away from the doorway, under a line of hanging baskets. He heard Aisling shuffling boxes somewhere in the back room.

'Who *is* that?' Sadie asked now.

'My godmother.'

Sadie's eyes widened, and then she frowned as if she was putting the pieces of a puzzle together.

'I love you,' he whispered, circling her waist, taking her by the hips. She always had fitted against him just perfectly. 'I'm in love with you, Sadie Mills, and it's all your fault for making me miss you so very badly while I was away in America.'

Her eyes clouded over, misty with tears. He attempted to dry them, but it didn't work.

'I thought love was a waste of time...' she said after a moment.

Her voice was broken, but she was looking at him as she'd never looked at him before, and it made his heart expand to the size of a football.

'Not our kind of love,' he said.

He was surprised at the words now falling so effortlessly from his mouth. She was right. If they hadn't been such good friends first, things never would have reached this point of trust... of no going back.

'We will never end. I won't let us. Never. I'm tying you up in chains...'

'To your bed, I hope?' she teased.

'If that's what you'd prefer.'

Owen lowered his lips to hers for a second time, open-mouthed. Her tongue was hungry, but soft, like velvet treacle sliding seductively across his, and he responded to her sensuous kisses again and again. Her hands were in his hair now, her fingers caressing the back of his neck, and as he kept on kissing her and kissing her he felt the fire in his veins, the spark of the start of something he knew he would never let die out. He would burn for her until the day he died.

Four months later

Sadie caught Owen's eyes across the garden and he winked at her. He looked amusingly animated, talking with a cousin, and almost as handsome in his tux as he had been in that kilt. But unfortunately there were no hay-strewn barns at the unique waterfront location his dad's new wife had chosen for the wedding.

Nevertheless, the yacht club in Cornwall was a stunning yellow-brick venue, to the right of a half-moon sandy bay. She could not wait to get back to their historic hotel, to lie under the cool sheets with Owen. But that would come later... as would she, many times, if this morning's session was anything to go by.

'Are you glad you let me ask you to come here,

finally?' he teased, when he found her moments later, looping his arms around her from behind.

'Oh, absolutely.'

She leaned back against his chest and closed her eyes, smiling at how his being like this with her, doing 'boyfriend' things, made her feel. She felt like a goddess around him, and he wouldn't stop telling her how good she looked in her dress. And out of it.

'I was just wondering if your mother was going to show up,' she said.

Owen smiled into the top of her head. He'd told her about his father's last wedding, how his mother had been escorted out of the venue, but things were different now. For a start, she wasn't at this one.

'Even if she was here, I have a feeling she'd be OK,' he told her. 'She's been making a concerted effort to be happy for him lately. And me, too.'

He dropped a kiss to her head and she turned in his arms. Sadie knew her words to his mother had hit home. Apparently, she'd been quite impressed with her, and had been asking after them as a couple ever since. While Sadie hadn't actually met her yet, it was only because she'd taken herself on a therapeutic trip to Borneo, to relax around orangutans—something she'd always wanted to do.

'She finally admitted she'd never fallen out

of love him—can you believe that?' Owen said. 'They actually spoke like civilised beings. My dad apologised...he even asked her here. She said the orangutans were more civilised than the Penner men, but at least she smiled when she said it.'

'Well, if you need me to talk to anyone here, I have a few *nice* things I can say about the Penner men,' she told Owen now, pulling him closer by the lapels of his jacket and pressing her lips to his.

He smiled under her kiss, which sent a wave of tingles through her belly to her lacy underwear. She would never get enough of this feeling. Her best friend and her boyfriend, all in one unbelievable package.

Of course people here were talking. They'd never seen Owen with a girlfriend before. He'd warned her in advance what people might say. But it wasn't as if that fazed her—not any more. They both knew what they'd built together was unshakable.

It had been strange at first, leaving Scotland and heading back to their normal lives. Only, now 'normal' was so much better. Owen had pretty much moved into her place. They were taking some time out from work to plan their next adventure—potentially spending some time in Thailand, as Owen had planned before—and then a couple's work placement in a medical team on a cruise ship in the Caribbean. Everything was exciting. Anything felt possible.

'I want your best friend benefits to myself... should we get out of here?' he whispered now, as the band started up next to the dance floor.

She frowned up at him. 'You're not even going to ask me to dance?'

'That depends. Will you stay on the dance floor or will you run away?'

'Very funny.'

Surrounded by wedding guests and in front of his rather shocked-looking father, Sadie kissed him in the confetti swirls and made a point to explain—again—how she was sober this time, and was not about to dash away and be sick.

He laughed, of course, sweeping her up in his arms and spinning her around until she told him that, OK, she might be sick after all.

Ugh! To think he'd felt the same back then! And neither of them had followed up on it!

Not that she would have been ready... It had taken all these years for her to be ready for Owen, she thought, letting the music carry her mind elsewhere. It had taken all this time for him to be ready for her, too.

Her parents loved him, of course. They'd all gone away for a weekend, to the Lake District, where they'd laughed and cried and talked openly about Chris. It had felt so freeing, after all this time, not to carry guilt or shame, just to remember her brother as the amazing guy she'd grown up with.

She had to admit it had been nice to see her mother laughing and snuggling against her father again, too. Even nicer that she'd been able to do the same with Owen, knowing she could laugh or cry and he'd be there, like he always was.

She'd never said *I love you* so many times, and she still felt the buzz and the butterflies. Just waking up in his arms was enough to make her start every day with the kind of joy she'd thought belonged only to children's television presenters. It was, as Parminder had joked when she'd video called them last week, *'Quite disgusting to witness.'*

Parminder had thought they might both like to know that they'd finally located the source of the banging in the walls at Rothesay. It was not a horrible haunting, as some people had loved to imagine, but rather a family of squirrels!

Secretly Sadie was glad she hadn't known that before—not because she enjoyed the thought of ghosts, but because seeing Owen with Parminder that night had woken something up in her...some dormant attraction to her best friend and the jealousy that had forced her to address what she really wanted in a partner.

'*Now* can we get out of here?'

Owen's whisper in her ear sent a shiver through her shoulder blades and she realised she'd zoned out on the dance floor, her head on his shoulder, moving to a slow song. A lazy smile crept over her face. This was her best friend, through and through—impatient, keen to move on to the next good thing. Only this time, and every single time going forward, she was going *with* him.

* * * * *

*If you enjoyed this story, check out
these other great reads from
Becky Wicks*

**The Vet's Escape to Paradise
A Princess in Naples
White Christmas with Her Millionaire Doc
Fling with the Children's Heart Doctor**

All available now!